BETWEEN A ROCK AND A HARD PLACE

The Honorable Judge Sherman O'Dell rubbed his sweaty palms together and said, "There's a promoter named Willie Crush planning a big railroad to-do. He's with the Katy rail line, and he's fast-talked them into staging a big crash—duel of the iron monsters they're calling it. It's gonna take place in a new town just west of here. Town's gonna need a new marshall and you could be it."

Ken Farley hated himself for it, but his heart leapt in his chest. "My badge is a little tarnished, isn't it, Sherm?" he asked.

"Or by tomorrow," Judge Sherman O'Dell continued, "you could be dead!"

ERNEST HAYCOX
IS THE KING OF THE WEST!

Over twenty-five million copies of Ernest Haycox's rip-roaring western adventures have been sold worldwide! For the very finest in straight-shooting western excitement, look for the Pinnacle brand!

RIDERS WEST (17-123-1, $2.95)
by Ernest Haycox
Neel St. Cloud's army of professional gunslicks were fixing to turn Dan Bellew's peaceful town into an outlaw strip. With one blazing gun against a hundred, Bellew found himself fighting for his valley's life—and for his own!

MAN IN THE SADDLE (17-124-X, $2.95)
by Ernest Haycox
The combine drove Owen Merritt from his land, branding him a coward and a killer while forcing him into hiding. But they had made one drastic, fatal mistake: they had forgotten to kill him!

SADDLE AND RIDE (17-085-5, $2.95)
by Ernest Haycox
Clay Morgan had hated cattleman Ben Herendeen since boyhood. Now, with all of Morgan's friends either riding with Big Ben and his murderous vigilantes or running from them, Clay was fixing to put an end to the lifelong blood feud — one way or the other!

"MOVES STEADILY, RELENTLESSLY FORWARD WITH GRIM POWER."
— THE NEW YORK TIMES

Available wherever paperbacks are sold, or order direct from the Publisher. Send cover price plus 50¢ per copy for mailing and handling to Pinnacle Books, Dept. 17-298, 475 Park Avenue South, New York, N.Y. 10016. Residents of New York, New Jersey and Pennsylvania must include sales tax. DO NOT SEND CASH.

TEXAS TWISTER

DELL BEMAN

PINNACLE BOOKS
WINDSOR PUBLISHING CORP.

PINNACLE BOOKS

are published by

Windsor Publishing Corp.
475 Park Avenue South
New York, NY 10016

Copyright © 1988 by Dell Beman. Published by arrangement with M. Evans and Company, Inc. Originally published in hardcover as CRUSH.

All rights reserved. No part of this book may be reproduced in any form or by any means without the prior written consent of the Publisher, excepting brief quotes used in reviews.

First Pinnacle Books printing: September, 1989

Printed in the United States of America

Chapter One

Farley was out like a Boot Hill corpse when his jailers roused him. There were two of them, muttering to each other. They both had those high-pitched whines one hears in Texas sometimes, as if their vocal cords were strung tighter than banjo strings.

"Looks like a bum to me. You sure he's the lawman brought in the Slades?"

"Years back, in Wichita. It's him, all right. Farley Dant ... he sure ain't a big hero no more. Killer. Judge'll put a noose around his neck and hang him now, and I'm going to be there to see it." There was a sick glee in the man's rasping words.

"Town needs a hanging. Haven't had one in a month or so. Wonder why O'Dell wants to talk to him first. Think he used to know him?"

"You never can tell with the judge. All I know is, we'd better quit jawing and get him up."

Farley kept his head to the cell wall, listening, playing

possum. He opened one eye. It was half glued shut, gritty. The scenery wasn't great. Jail-cell walls all look alike. Straight off, Farley couldn't remember just where he was or what he had done. He knew he'd gotten drunk. His pounding head and dry, scuzzy mouth told him that. What was the talk of a hanging?

He felt a rough hand shaking his shoulder and stifled a curse. He wasn't ready to wake up and remember. The wheezing man—the one who had said he wanted to see the hanging—was about five paces away. Bad lungs. Farley knew the type. Every other man's death would make him happy, because it wasn't his—yet.

"Git up, killer," the one standing over Farley said. When that didn't work, he slammed Farley in the kidneys with a hard, tight fist. Farley hated a dirty fighter.

Without giving it much thought, Farley swung around on the narrow cot and aimed a punch at the man's crotch. Either he missed or Weasel Face had balls of cast iron, because he jumped back, grinning slyly. "I'll see you swing, too, Dant."

Bad Lungs slopped a basin of water on the cell floor, air hissing in and out of his chest with effort. "Get yourself cleaned up, you scummy bastard. Judge wants to see you in his chambers."

The barred door clicked shut, leaving Farley on the wrong side of it. The name O'Dell rolled through his numbed brain like the spinning pellet in a keno game, trying to find a place to light. He couldn't hook it up with a judge, though. Farley knew that name from somewhere, and he had a hunch it wasn't going to come up a winning number.

Unfortunately, other pictures were beginning to surface like low cards in a big game. None of them were good. Farley recalled upending the whiskey bottle after he'd shot Thaddeus Beauchamp through the heart. The rotgut had tasted a damned sight better than it did now, soured in his stomach.

A Peacemaker against a derringer, Farley recalled. Beauchamp didn't have much of a chance. Not that he didn't have it coming, after what he had done to Lottie Crystal. For once, fair was about as far from Farley's mind as Cripple Creek, where it had all begun with Lottie.

Farley had run out of places to go by the time he hit Cripple Creek. Funny how he was a big hero, and all of a sudden he wasn't anything anymore. He couldn't point to just when it happened, but it was like the boomtowns, all wild and free, and all of a sudden they were closed up and gray, smaller, dwarfed by the churches, maybe.

Not that Farley was against religion for someone else, but he damned sure didn't believe one group of men should decide what another group of men were and weren't going to do when it came to drinking, gaming, and womanizing.

Maybe that was just an excuse, though. The whiskey had gotten to Farley—and the memory of too many men he had faced down. Life had gone sour, until he had hooked up with Lottie. He had been so tired of killing, of men trying to prove themselves by outdrawing him, because he had had a name, once.

Ah, Lottie, he thought as he scrubbed listlessly with the cloth and cold water the jailers had left. *You were the queen of Cripple Creek, all right. Your own fancy house and all, girls, gaming, and the whole shebang, you had it all.*

I remember when you first looked at me there. Don't know why you took notice of a broken-down lawman hiding in a bottle ... but you did.

I was a good dealer, wasn't I, Lottie? Once you set me at it, I found my hands were as quick with cards as with a gun. And soon enough I had a living—and a friend.

I hadn't had a friend in a long time, Lottie, and you were a good one, sharing your bed, but most of all, sharing life. I was happy. You didn't ask nothing—didn't want to own me, and didn't want me possessing you.

Good years, Lottie, two of the best. Until that damned Thaddeus Beauchamp showed up, and I saw you looking at him with the same bright eyes I saw when you were looking me over the first time ...

Farley was remembering now, remembering at last through his booze stupor, what had brought him here to West, Texas. He was done with the scrubbing and buttoned his shirt.

Ah, Lottie, I saw that dandy, that gilt-edged gambler staring back at you and I just sank inside, hit bottom, knowing the kind of man he was, how he'd treat you, and how you'd end up. Saw it all right then. Soft-talking bastard but mean. He'd slap you around, call you a whore, never let you have an ounce of self-respect, make you a slave. Oh, I knew the type. I tried to warn you ... but you just smiled. Queen of Cripple Creek just smiled.

I quit the dealing then and just worked. Soon enough you sold the place, ran off with that tinhorn. He took your money, Lottie, and ditched you in Abilene, and you went down like a stone, sucking laudanum. . . .

He killed you, Lottie, and now I've killed him back. For you. Tracked him from Colorado to Kansas to the Nations to West, Texas. And shot the bastard at the poker table. Wanted to do that for a long time. Guess I'll hang for it, Lottie, but I wanted to. You gave me something even better than love. You gave me friendship.

Both Bad Lungs and Weasel Face escorted Farley out into the blinding sunlight, around the corner, and to the granite building that housed the judge's chambers. Weasel was holding the Colt .45 this time. Curious townsfolk gawked. Farley hoped none of them remembered him from way back.

The short walk started Farley sweating, and the bad booze popped out his pores and rolled off him in streams. His shirt stuck to his chest. When they got inside, he shivered with a sudden chill.

A big double door was done up in gilt lettering, real official-looking. It read, JUDGE'S CHAMBERS. Bad Lungs and Weasel Face shoved Farley through it, toward a fat man sitting behind an expanse of polished oak desk. The plaque in front of him read, THE HONORABLE JUDGE SHERMAN O'DELL.

The keno ball that had been rattling around in the back of Farley's head plunked to a stop on a losing number. But the Sherman O'Dell Farley had known had been slim and dapper and wily. Farley had learned from O'Dell, back then, that there was no honor among thieves.

Farley squinted. Today even the inside of a mine shaft would be too bright for him. He saw beady eyes watching him from an overfed porker's face. Fingers like overstuffed sausages stopped in midair, holding a fat, unlit cigar. One end was slimy with spit, and it had teeth marks on it.

Chins jiggled when the man's lips curled up, suggesting a sly, cunning look. A gash in the head turns upward at the corners, and the eyes peer out flat and mean, waiting. Farley remembered that look. It was the same O'Dell, all right, beneath the layers of suet.

The old tub of lard has done all right for himself, Farley thought. Maybe O'Dell was cleverer than Farley had ever given him credit for. He had bamboozled a whole town if he was a judge now. It wasn't fair, but O'Dell looked prosperous. Oily but prosperous. Once, Farley could have shot him, if he hadn't been so sick of killing.

"You boys can go," O'Dell told the jailers. "Wait outside."

"But this one's murder," Bad Lungs wheezed.

"Outside—and shut the door behind you," O'Dell said so softly, Farley could hardly hear him. The two men scrambled over each other like scared rabbits rushing to obey. Interesting.

"Sit yourself down, Dant," O'Dell ordered, gesturing to a straight-backed chair on the other side of the desk.

Farley sat. He tilted the chair back on two legs and screeched the worn heels of his boots along the polished floor before they caught, bracing him. He yawned loudly. He plucked the judge's plaque up off the desk, handling it like it was a stinkbug he'd like to squash if he didn't know better.

"Never thought I'd see you fat and sassy on that side of the law, Sherm. Glad they wrote it out for me, or I wouldn't believe my own eyes. People around these parts know about you, before you became the Honorable?"

"Dead men don't talk," O'Dell said. He chuckled. Farley couldn't hear any fun in it. "Looks like you won't get a chance to, either, if we hang you tomorrow."

"You haven't made up your mind yet?" Farley asked. He hoped he sounded cool and unruffled. Hanging was not the way he wanted to go. He'd seen enough of it, the way the muscles twitched, jerked in a last spasm, and were still, the way flies crowded the swollen tongue.

"I'm thinking on it," O'Dell said slowly. "I heard all about Lottie Crystal and how you were avenging her. Might get you off, if she was a wife or a proper woman instead of a shady lady. But hell, Dant, this is 1896. That 'vengeance-is-mine' ballyhoo doesn't wash with the citizens anymore."

Farley's eyes hurt some from the glitter bounding off O'Dell's pinkie ring, a flashy diamond set in gold, but his gaze followed the movement. Farley had trained himself to watch a man's hands and his eyes at the same time. Sometimes it had saved his life.

Sherman O'Dell's fat fingers were as busy as ten grubs, fondling the sheet on Beauchamp, twinkling down to a desk drawer to extract a decanter and two shot glasses. His shiny brown eyes gazed at Beauchamp's sheet. He acted nervous. Could he be remembering he owed Farley one? "The man you killed was a crooked gambler and a scalawag, but he wasn't a killer. So what am I supposed to do?"

"Knowing you, Sherm, you'll do the right thing," Farley said. He couldn't stop the contempt that roiled beneath the surface of his words.

"I could hang you, all right. Here in West, I am the law—the law east of the Pecos, eh?" Farley knew in that instant that Judge Roy Bean's domain stung O'Dell, even at this distance. Roy Bean had a regular empire out there.

But what did that have to do with Farley, a prisoner sitting here just out of reach of that whiskey bottle, being played along like a prize pig at a fair? O'Dell wanted something, but damn if Farley could figure out what.

"But as I said, maybe we could find some way around this problem, some way that would help us both. I don't think it would make me real popular, not with the folks who remember when you brought in the Slades, if I was to hang you."

Don't let him get you, Farley told himself. He knew how Sherm's mind worked, twisting and turning things around, looking for a weak spot. Farley couldn't show he was scared.

"That was ten years ago, Sherm. I don't often remember it myself. But if I was to, I might remember that a man who looked something like you was riding with them. He got away."

Sherm stroked his chin. "Is that a fact?"

Farley watched his own leathery hands drumming his

side of the desk as if they belonged to someone else. He hoped O'Dell did not see them trembling.

O'Dell cradled the whiskey decanter as if warming his hands with its amber promise. He picked it up as if he were about to pour, and clanked it back down. Relief was just out of Farley's reach. Farley knew he was being watched, knew the beady eyes were looking him over. He wondered if it showed, how much he was itching for that shot. He needed one right now.

Farley tried not to think about it. He was tired of O'Dell's fat face, tired of whatever game O'Dell was playing this time. There wasn't any sense in dragging it on, in bouncing whatever it was back and forth. It might be O'Dell's way, but it wasn't Farley's. "Cut the bull and flat out tell me what you have in mind. And I'll give you a yes or no, with no hard feelings."

"Okay," Sherm said, rubbing his sweaty palms together like he was about to deal a hand of cards—a stacked deck—knowing beforehand that he was going to win. "There's a man named Willie Crush, planning a big railroad to-do. No, not outlaw. Promoter. He's with the Katy rail line, and he's fast-talked them into staging a big crash. Duel of the iron monsters, they're calling it. And it's going to take place within spitting distance of West. We're calling the town Crush, after Willie, and that's a fact.

"I guess I don't have to tell you, I already have the town of West in my pocket—but there's not enough here for a man with ambition, if you follow me. No fast money and damned few fast women. Now, Crush, that's a different story, and my name's on just about every plate, except the ones Willie has.

"But right off, we're not sure about a town developing. What we are sure of is that it's going to be boomtown for a day. Well, for a couple weeks, with one big day. Lots of action. Folks from all along the Katy rail line from as far away as Parsons, Kansas, to Galveston, Texas, are going to be coming to see the event, the big crash. They are going to run special excursion trains. A promotion like that is bound to be worth a fortune, if a man plays his cards right. And I'm going to be in on it."

Farley cut in. "I get the idea. You don't have to sell me. You plan to run this boomtown and get something out of it. What I don't get is where I fit in."

"Town's going to need a marshal, and you could be it," Sherm said. "Or come tomorrow, you could be dead."

Farley hated himself for it, but his heart leapt in his chest. He kept telling himself that he didn't much care if he lived or died, but his heart said he lied.

O'Dell was offering him some sort of trade, but what sort of rope would he be trading the hangman's noose for? Farley wondered. He hated the old lard-ass, always had—and O'Dell knew it.

I might be a drunk sometimes, but I've never robbed or swindled anyone, Farley thought. *O'Dell is up to something big, but what the hell is it? It's not as simple as it looks, my life against acting as marshal for this Crush. And why me? Does he know why that bullet missed him, way back?*

It took an effort for Farley to keep his voice steady. "My badge is a little tarnished for modern-day marshal, don't you think, Sherm?"

"Maybe, maybe not." O'Dell tossed a wanted poster across the desk. It was of a bank robber named Deadeye Dick. O'Dell didn't need to explain. The bandit looked enough like Beauchamp to be his double.

O'Dell's laugh sent a chill up Farley's spine. "You could be a big hero if the man you shot down was Deadeye Dick. The papers would love you, and they'd be mighty impressed if Crush were to hire you as lawman. I've always wanted to *own* a hero myself...."

"Let's get one thing straight, Sherm. No one owns me. Never has and never will."

Brave words, hero, Farley thought wryly, feeling the hope and fear twist in his gut.

"If that's the way you want it," Sherm said, rising from his chair, taking the wanted poster from Farley's hands, "we can forget the whole thing. Maybe I forgot, since we go a long way back, that we never were friends."

Farley could feel his throat tighten, could almost feel the way the noose would scratch against his neck. A strangling noise escaped him, and Sherm heard it, knew what it meant.

O'Dell pounced and grabbed Farley by the collar. He pulled him close, so Farley's washed-out blue eyes stared into O'Dell's round, shiny ones. He spit out his words. "What's it to be, Farley, dead man or hero? And I'll tell you right now, if you choose hero, I expect you to be grateful when the time comes."

Farley felt his face grow hot. O'Dell was calling his bluff and he was ashamed of his hand—and even more ashamed of the way he was going to play it. He whispered hoarsely, "Does a shot of whiskey seal the deal, Sherm?"

O'Dell dropped the bunched fabric of Farley's shirt. He sat down in his chair with that smile of his that wasn't a smile at all. He poured two shots of whiskey and handed Farley one, raising his own in a toast. "To the marshal of Crush, Texas," he said. "May his brief days of glory be profitable for both of us."

Farley drank. It was better than shaking hands.

Chapter Two

Amelia Bloomer McCoy drew herself up to her full five-foot-six—unusually tall, but her mother had believed in red meat, celery tonic, and raw vegetables, as well as the vote for women—and extended her two dollars in paper money with a gloved hand.

"A ticket to Crush, Texas," she said firmly.

The visored ticket agent eyed her with mistrust. Even at a glance she looked different from the women he was used to dealing with. Those he could classify in a second: either pallid saints prone to vapors or she-devil sinners. Secretly he favored the latter, but his wife belonged to the First Baptist Church of Dallas.

"There ain't no such place on my list," he told her.

"My good man," Amelia said, pointing to the garish advertisement on the wall of the train station, "that clearly says that there is an excursion train to Crush, and the cost is listed. Now, if you please, my ticket."

The agent blushed. This female had looked him directly

in the eye as she contradicted him. He shuffled his feet and dropped his gaze, but not before he noted her eyes were like those of a cat, an almost clear amber shot through with flecks of green.

She didn't look like a bad woman. Worse luck. He was not averse to a little titillation in his day. Her dark hair was neatly drawn back, and she wore one of those newfangled shirtwaists. Easterner, probably. And if there was one breed he had no use for, it was Easterners.

"If you look closer, ma'am, that there bill says there's gonna be a town named Crush, and when it gets around to being a town, you can buy a ticket. Two weeks from today, and that's a fact. Or, likely, I can sell you a ticket for when there's gonna be a town and a train goin' to it." He scratched his nose. He had handled that rather well, he thought.

"But I want to go there this week," Amelia said.

"There ain't no town, and there ain't no train stops there, ma'am," he repeated. "Now, if you want to go to Waco or West or somewheres, maybe I can help."

"But surely, sir, the railroad line passes Crush."

"Well, it does, but it don't. There is no Crush, rightly speaking." This one certainly was persistent. Maybe one of those fancy women trying to play proper lady? From what the conductor out of Waco told him, there was plenty going on at the site for the great Crush train crash. Maybe she did want to go there now?

"And if there is a line, surely the train can stop and let me off," Amelia said.

Just then a man in a bowler hat strode up to the counter and demanded, "Ticket to Crush."

Ignoring his rudeness, Amelia turned to him and asked, "Sir, perhaps you can help me convince this clerk that tickets to Crush can be made available."

Before the end of the day the bewildered agent had issued tickets for the following morning's train, with a special stop thirty miles outside West, to a dozen passengers.

Besides Amelia, the purchasers were two ladies the ticket agent knew for sure were scarlet women, though both called themselves Smith; three shifty-eyed gambling types; four carpenters and general tradesmen; a man whose face he could have sworn he had seen recently in the papers; and a prizefight promoter. Crush was already booming.

The train was raising dust south of Dallas by the time Amelia got a good look at her closest traveling companions. The mutton-chopped conductor, who had herded the special Crush passengers into coach number five, had placed her opposite the two Smith women. They were clearly not related except in the sisterhood of their profession. Their low-cut satin traveling suits drew admiring glances.

Several of the men had tried to help Amelia lug her daguerreo-type camera up the swaying aisle, but she had shooed them away. By employing her grip and kicking her overstuffed valise forward with her feet, she had managed herself. She gave the scowling conductor a brief, triumphant nod.

She propped the wooden box up beside her like a mother tending a baby. The clumsy tripod she stuffed under the rattan bench, beside her auxiliary equipment. She also carried a portable Hawk-Eye, the newest and smallest of the detective and combination cameras, with her.

The Smiths, Evelyn and Clara, according to their tickets, had been shooting daggers at each other, assessing future competition. Now they turned their combined hostility on Amelia. The chill was palpable.

"Lovely morning, isn't it, ladies?" Amelia said, to let them know she was not one of those judgmental Bible thumpers.

Clara, whose brash red hair clashed violently with the peacock feathers in her broad-brimmed hat, gave in to her curiosity. "You bringing all that stuff to your husband all by yourself?" she asked. Evelyn kicked her in the shins.

"No," Amelia said. "I am, myself, a working woman." The Smith women guffawed. Amelia raised her chin defiantly. "My mother was a Bloomer, and my sister is a Pinkerton agent, and I am a photographer." Then she lowered her voice and added, "My mother was married, of course."

"You mean, you don't have a husband but you're looking," Evelyn said with a snort. "Some a lot older and plainer than you do all right out West."

In the conversational void the hissing of the steam engine grew louder. Amelia felt her face grow hot. She might be on the far side of twenty-five but she was still on the right side of thirty. Barely ... but her beaus back East had considered her attractive. Or was the latest compliment "intellectually stimulating?"

Amelia reminded herself that she needed to make friends with all elements of society and stifled a sharp retort. She forced a weak smile. "Marriage doesn't interest me," she said. "Pictures do. I intend to record some bald truths about the so-called heroic West."

"Like in them fancy magazines about outlaws and lawmen?" Clara asked, sighing. "Heroes."

"Not exactly," Amelia said. "It is my contention that these men are not always heroes. In fact, a sensible woman could get thoroughly sick of the eulogizing in the New York *Telegraph*, and even *Colliers*. These famous marshals are often rapacious creatures as violent as their opponents."

"You sure use big words," Evelyn sniffed.

"Well, what I mean is, I want to show these men as they really are, destroying land and animals, building their little boomtowns, killing other men, strutting around like banty roosters...."

Clara's peacock feathers danced when she giggled. "I think I know what you're talkin' about. One time this woman I worked for showed me this fancy piece on Bat Masterson, about how brave he was and all. Well, this madam, she tells me, 'Bat was a customer of mine, way back when I was flat-backing. And he dropped his drawers, same as any other man....' "

Amelia tried to hold her face stern and blush, to concentrate on the rolling landscape outside the window, but the effort defeated her. Her lips twitched, her cheeks wriggled, and an ear-to-ear grin exploded. "That's it," she managed to say between great barking fits of laughter. "That's exactly what I mean!"

"Bat Masterson dropping his drawers!" Evelyn howled.

The three women laughed long and loud. Every time

they tried to straighten up, new gales assailed them. Tears streamed down their faces.

Finally, Clara's curiosity overtook her again. "Could you really get pictures like you're talking about? True pictures, I mean, not just some man's ... ha, ha! Well, you can't just go up to some lawman—"

"Marshal Dant," Evelyn said, cutting in. "He's the big shot out at Crush. Killed a big-time bank robber named Deadeye Dick, not long back."

Amelia noticed the man in the newly trimmed black beard turn his head slightly, so as not to miss a word. But by then all the other passengers were eavesdropping and shaking their heads over this strange Eastern lady carrying on with a couple of whores.

"I have some new inventions with me," Amelia explained, telling Evelyn and Clara about the continuous-roll film a fellow named Carbutt had developed. She showed them her new camera, a lightweight contraption that fit in the palm of her hand, and promised to take their pictures later, in Crush.

"We'll be working at Dant's Saloon and Dance Hall," Clara said. "Least, that's where *I'll* be working."

"I also have a special invitation to work there," Evelyn informed her with a smile so syrupy that if sweetness could kill, Clara would be rolling over dead right now. "A very dear friend of mine, a judge, set it up for me."

"Before or after he fined you?" That had been too good for Clara to let go.

"Hmm. You might have had trouble with the law where you came from, but I got the law on my side in Crush.

Judge Sherman O'Dell practically owns the town, you know."

Amelia's mind raced for a safe subject before the two Smiths tore into each other. "Tell me about Crush, please," she said. "It sounds like such a ... Western gesture, to build a town for a train crash." She didn't add that her Uncle Sylvester, a journalist by vocation and gambler by avocation, had hinted that Crush would become newsworthy.

Clara and Evelyn filled her in on what they knew. The false-front saloon had been hastily erected just last week, and girls chased out of other towns were headed there to work. It was a darned shame, but life in most Kansas, Oklahoma, and Texas towns were getting so settled, a woman had trouble making an honest living.

Crush promised to be different, almost like a three-week carnival. This Judge O'Dell and Marshal Dant seemed to be making the most of a brief season, and rumor had it that gambling was wide open. Then, too, besides the "duel of the iron monsters" people would flock by the thousands to see, rumor had it that something else was going to happen, something big, though Evelyn wasn't sure just what.

"And where there's that many hot-blooded men, honey," Clara concluded, "I reckon I can do all right."

"For a redhead," Evelyn said, patting her own cap of golden curls. "I've found most men are partial to blondes."

"I'm sure you'll both be very popular," Amelia said, almost choking on her words. She wondered if she ought to mention dignity, unity, and the vote for women now, or wait.

"Some men might go for the gold," Clara said, "but the way I understand it, Farley Dant favors redheads."

They were still arguing the issue by late afternoon when the train braked in the middle of what had been, until recently, a dusty cotton field.

By then Amelia had learned a lot about the past and present exploits of the great lawman, Farley Dant. She was pleased. Not only had she made friends with the two dance hall girls, but also she had targeted her man.

And just as soon as she got settled, she intended to shoot. She fondled her Hawk-Eye in anticipation.

"You sure you want to get out at this hellhole?" the conductor asked Amelia. "Train goes on to Waco, and there's another one back to Dallas...."

Amelia heaved her valise to the ground in answer. It kicked up a cloud of dust. She was not sure. Two slick fellows with nervous eyes had whisked Evelyn and Clara away with them, baggage and all. Amelia was the last passenger to depart from coach number five, and no eager hands reached out to help her. In fact, her fellow travelers had fled from her as if avoiding a cholera plague.

"Least let me help you with this here heavy box," the conductor said. His breath hissed in with effort and disapproval, and together they struggled with the daguerreotype camera. He piled it beside Amelia, who stood forlornly in the midst of her possessions.

He shouted his parting words over the loud chugging

of the departing locomotive, hanging his head out the door and grasping the handrail. "Ain't no place for a proper lady, even if she does chat up with hoors...."

Silently Amelia agreed. Crush did not look promising. The September heat sent dust-laden waves shimmering from the ground. The sound of hammers reverberated through the heavy air, and the entire settlement smelled of the dried horse manure cobbling the new streets. The fresh odor of sawdust from the half-constructed train platform did not mask a general lack of amenities.

Amelia felt rivulets of perspiration trickling down her sides under her navy blue serge jacket. She had wanted to find a raw boomtown, and her idea for a pictorial essay had sounded fine and noble in the drawing rooms of New York. Now, confronting the reality, she longed for a bath.

Nearby, a workman gawked at her, but not one of them rushed to her aid. The town—a slipshod collection of tents and buildings on up ahead—looked like a tawdry mirage, out of reach. Amelia paused and asked herself what her sister, Victoria, would do in a situation like this.

Then, gathering herself up to her full height, she strode over and said loudly to the man without a hammer or planks, the one she assumed was boss, "I will give one of your men a silver dollar to escort me to the hotel."

The pounding ceased abruptly. Amelia caught the glint of a hammer paused in midair. The entire crew snickered at her, except for the foreman. He told her gravely, "Ain't no hotel, ma'am."

"Boardinghouse?"

"Not exactly. Maybe next week, but right now, ain't no hotel and ain't no boardinghouse...."

"And ain't no town," Amelia muttered.

"What's that, ma'am?"

"Nothing," Amelia said, exasperated. "Perhaps you could suggest someplace that might rent a room to a woman, Mr. . . . ?"

"Silas Clute, ma'am. And no, ma'am, I couldn't rightly recommend a place to a lady of ... er, a certain breeding."

"Mr. Clute, I am standing here in the middle of nowhere without a roof over my head, looking at buildings and tents and people who surely must stay in them. Surely you can recommend something."

"Yes, ma'am. We could flag the Dallas train for you tomorrow," Clute said, wiping his forehead with a greasy handkerchief. "Or more than likely, you could find somebody to ride you into West, not more'n half a day's ride, where there is a hotel and a train stop."

Suddenly the afternoon heat seemed to have gone up several degrees. Amelia felt a new tack was necessary. "Where will the women who got off the train here stay, Mr. Clute?"

Fresh sweat beaded Clute's broad forehead, which was turning a dusky purple color. "Those kind of women stay at Dant's, same as anybody who can pay the price, but it ain't no place for a lady."

"Mr. Clute," Amelia said, trying to make her voice forceful, "for the moment, please forget that I am a lady"—several of the hands hooted at that—"and consider me a photographer with a job to do, the same as any other ... person. Where would you recommend I stay?"

The foreman blinked his beady eyes, twisted his sodden

kerchief, and finally offered, "Well, I can take you on up to Dant's, but I can't promise nothing. Boys, you want to knock off for the day? Can't trust you after I leave, anyway."

Whoops and hollers answered him. Five overheated, ripe construction workers, with Amelia and Clute in the lead, trooped down the gash of red clay toward town. A handpainted sign, already pocked with bullet holes, declared that the passageway was named Broadway. Amelia refrained from asking whether it was a street or an avenue.

She lifted her long skirts and high-stepped every time she crossed a plop of horse dung. Her upturned nose wrinkled up, but she plowed on. In all her dreams about frontier towns she had never once considered the sanitation problems. Nor had Victoria mentioned it in her letters about the West, though the word *primitive* had cropped up from time to time. Horse manure, Amelia concluded, was primitive.

Nameless faces, all male, peered at Amelia and her entourage from the flaps of crude tents and the darkened entranceways of shacks. Thus far, there was only one decent-sized building completed along Broadway, Dant's Saloon and Dance Hall. A scrawled sign announced: & JAIL and U.S. POST OFFICE.

"Just temporary," Silas Clute told her. "Jail'll be finished soon, and the shebang will handle the mail, ma'am."

He pointed with pride to the studs and rafters that would become the General Emporium and post office. He indicated that the square area, now cordoned off with builder's string, would become an arena for some fine entertainment. "*That* the gentlemen will enjoy," he added when Amelia raised her eyebrows.

Amelia favored him with a genuine smile, touched. He was rough and sweaty, but he was trying to act like a gentleman. And although Amelia had found that well-meaning gentlemen could be a hindrance, she needed a friend right now.

"You wait out here, ma'am, while I see if Marshal Dant's in the saloon," Silas Clute said.

No doubt the man was also ready for a quick snort. Amelia could spot the signs, the slight twitch in the hands, the eagerness around the mouth, the bright anticipation in the eyes. She was by no means a Carry Nation, but she had uncles and a father. She knew.

After several minutes she began to tap her foot impatiently—after first checking out the territory beneath her high-buttoned shoes. She hated to hide behind trousers, and she hated waiting on men. Her mother had taught her to fight her own battles.

"I shall go in and inquire myself," she finally announced.

"In there!" A chorus from behind her sounded. The curious workmen were still with her.

Amelia stared at the swinging, batwing saloon doors. To the left about twelve feet was another, less imposing door. Judging from the plate-glass windows and the second story, it led to rooms for hire. "In there," she replied, and marched decisively toward it.

She ran smack into a flushed medicine drummer emerging with a dance hall girl on his arm. "Excuse me," she said. The girl glared at her.

28

Amelia sensed the construction workers, standing gaping in the so-called street, stiffen as she tried the door. It swung open. Inside, her vision adjusted to the dimness, and she saw a gnarled man behind a counter, bent over a ledger.

"I wish to rent a room," she said.

The man pushed at his wire-rimmed spectacles, as if having trouble with his eyesight or with what he was seeing. He harrumphed. His wizened face was as wrinkled as parchment. "You one of Dant's women?" he asked. His voice rose querulously.

"No, I certainly am not."

"Well, then, I don't think this is the place for you."

"My good sir," Amelia began, and immediately regretted her own politeness. She must be firm. The situation, as she saw it, was becoming desperate. "I wish to rent a room, and I know you have rooms available. Quite a few rooms, from the look of it. So do not shilly-shally, sir." She slammed her bag on the counter and extracted her purse. "Name your price and rent me a room. Immediately."

"Can't do that without talking to Farley Dant," the man said, bending his face low over the ledger again, hiding. "And Dant's in West until tomorrow."

Just then Silas Clute rushed in. "I can get you a ride to West, ma'am, but Farley Dant's out of town, and nobody wants to be responsible for renting you a room."

Amelia was so frustrated, she could scream. She considered the idea for a moment, then discarded it. She had a feeling that between the lizardlike man behind the counter and the sweaty foreman, they could outmaneuver her.

So, although she was not given to vapors, she began to moan. "Oh, the heat. If only I could lie down for a moment...."

As she sank to the floor, adjusting her skirt gracefully so it wouldn't billow up above her ankles, she recalled some of her mother's sage advice: as a last resort, act like a man thinks a woman ought to act.

And in truth it was quite pleasant to feel Clute's strong arms carry her upstairs to room number thirteen while one of his hired hands took care of her equipment. Once that was safely inside, beside the brass-railed bed, Amelia felt it was safe to flutter her eyelids and wink at Silas before saying thank you.

She was, after all, a lady.

Chapter Three

Farley had just missed Amelia earlier that day.

"Just put that whiskey bottle out here," Farley had told Gus, his barkeep. "I reckon a man needs a few belts for the trail."

"Going into West?" Gus said casually. He was catching on to the weekly routine. "What if those new girls show up today? They coming in by train?"

"Far as I know. If they do, put them to work and I'll catch up with them later. Got banking business. I reckon I'll be back tonight—no sense staying over. You can handle everything?"

"Colt's always loaded," Gus promised. "Might be easier if you'd make it official and deputize me, but I can manage."

"Hah, wish I could," Farley said. "Seems like we got deputies coming from West in a few days or so. I'd sooner have the women. Well"—Farley drank deeply, shuddered, and slammed his glass down—"until later."

Farley managed this weekly trip a lot better with a few belts under him. And why not? It was his saloon, or, in reality, ten percent of it was. And if he chose to slop up some of the profits, it was a damned sight better than facing these conferences with O'Dell stone-cold sober.

In the mornings—the only time Farley came close to being clearheaded, though he was almost always fuzzy-eyed and shaking like a dog shitting peach seeds—he felt like a hundred-year-old whore who'd hired out for two bits a throw.

Those belts, plus the flask he rode with for emergencies, saw Farley through to West in a tolerable glow that he sometimes mistook for peace.

Within spitting distance was still a hard ride across open territory. Nothing between Crush and West but rail tracks, rolling hills, some cotton fields and stands of mesquite. Pretty country in a way, and a long way from Cripple Creek.

Maybe it was not so bad.

But, Farley was always sorry when the weekly ride was over and he reached West. Something inside him plunked down lower than a snake's belly when he reined his horse in and slowed it to a walk.

He knew O'Dell was through at the granite courthouse for the day—Sherm didn't believe in working late. So Farley had to meet O'Dell at Blanche's, on the outskirts of the other side of town.

Blanche Walker was O'Dell's current paramour, a rounded widow quickly turning to plain fat. Farley'd wondered what the attraction was, until O'Dell told him, "Blanche's late husband just happened to leave her a heap of land, and some of it just happens to spill over into the new town of Crush. Might as well combine business and pleasure, eh?"

Farley remembered O'Dell's smirk over that as he rode up to the gimcrack, white-painted house with a picket fence outside and doilies cluttering the horsehair sofas inside.

"In here, Dant," called O'Dell.

Blanche was behind him, coming to the door. She wore that hot and humid look that came from more than the weather. "How nice to see you, Marshal Dant," she said, simpering.

I bet. You're still bulging out of those widow weeds like a sausage busted out of its casing. Been romping around with the other old tub of lard, huh? The thought of you and Sherm doing it about makes me want to swear off for life. "Howdy, Missus Walker."

Blanche fussed. "Howdy, indeed. That's all I get out of you two boys, then you're off discussing business. Well, Sherm sure is a smart one, taking care of things he says I can't bother my pretty little head about." About here in Blanche's speech, which varied little from week to week, Farley always felt ill. "I got the study all nice and cozy for you two."

"What a great little lady, eh?" Sherm O'Dell said, patting Blanche on the rump. She giggled. Coming from a corpulent woman with hair like barbed wire, it was not girlish. "Come on, Dant. I got appointments later."

So Farley followed. The late Mr. Walker's study was well appointed, tucked at the back of the house. No doilies here, only the clean lines of cured wood, a wide oak desk, and bookshelves crammed with volumes Blanche had never read, which made Farley aware, once again, of how hard smart women were to come by out here. Lottie had been a smart one, even read books.

Sherm turned to the sideboard and the brandy bottle. "Guess you're still slopping it down," he grunted.

"No more'n you, from what I've seen," Farley said curtly.

"Well, a man's drinking is his own business—I'll be the first to go along with that. Just keep yourself sharp enough to count the money, eh? What was the take last week?"

Farley had hand-carried the money bag—the weekly take from Dant's Saloon and Dance Hall—all the way from Crush. He slapped it across the desk. "You count it, it's all there. You know I'm an honest man."

Setting the filled brandy glasses down—he always made Farley reach for his—Sherm grabbed greedily for the loot. The jiggling of coins was muted by the rustle of paper money. If Sherm didn't like taking all that paper, it was his tough luck. O'Dell kept pointing out that it was 1896.

"Better'n last week," he said, his brown eyes shining more brightly. "Seems like we're building us a sweet little town. I plan to do some visiting, all right. I sent over those sisters of joy I was telling you about, only I reckon I'll have to come over and claim my piece of them, heh?"

"Thought you and the widow had a hot deal going," Farley said. He knew that would make O'Dell squirm. "Maybe even wedding bells, from what she told me last week."

Counting money always put O'Dell in a trance. It was hard to break through to him when his hands were fondling money; his lips sort of drooled at the corners. Farley'd gotten through to him. O'Dell shifted in his seat behind the desk. The chair groaned underneath him.

"Don't you get smart with me, Dant, you hear? No man alive can tell me he hasn't had a pig in the poke once in a while—including you. But between you and me, the only bells old Blanche is going to hear are those from the poorhouse."

"Shall I tell her that?"

"You repeat a word and you might find yourself strung up. Don't get uppity with me, Dant. I still know the truth about you and Beauchamp, and I can make it public easy enough."

"Spoken like a true gentleman."

"I never said I was. What's your beef, anyway? You get your ten percent for the week. You can't tell me *you* don't have a hot deal going."

"Yes, it's all right. Saloon's doing a good business, getting better all the time. Silas Clute is building away. He seems like a good man, which is why I want to know what he's doing working for you. Further, isn't it about time you let me in on what's going on there?"

"Why, Dant," O'Dell said, getting oily again, "you know as well as I do. We got the whorehouse going, and the gambling, and the train crash coming up."

"I didn't figure it's whores going to be sporting in that arena you're building. That's going a little far, even for you."

"That a fact? How far along is it? Why'd you say 'arena'? What's it look like?"

"Looks like a stage going up with lots of bleachers all

around. It's far enough along, so I can tell it has nothing to do with the duel of the iron monsters. It's away from the railroad hoopla, and it's going to be big. What are you planning?"

Sherm stroked his triple chins. "Thought they'd be plenty of time to fill you in on that little side deal. It looks big, maybe, but it's fair and square."

"Nothing you do is fair and square."

"Couldn't I have changed, eh? Well, it's nothing to fret about. In fact, I was meaning to talk to you about a business associate of mine who's going to show up. I want you to be right friendly to him. Man's name is Clive Gorman, from back East. He's a sharp operator, real sharp."

"And just what does this Clive Gorman do? Rob banks? Hold up women and children?"

"Heh, heh! Some mouth on you, Dant. A mouth like that could get a man strung up, eh? Clive's in the business of promoting a little gentlemen's entertainment. Just something for the folks who aren't that thrilled about seeing two locomotives crash."

"What sort of entertainment you got in mind?"

"Well, Dant, it's like this. You remember that big fracas when Bat Masterson tried to raise some money a while back?"

Farley remembered, all right. "You can't get away with it."

"Well, I think I'm maybe smarter than old Bat, trying to run things from a sports desk up in New York City. That was his problem—no control over the local situation, if you get my drift."

Suddenly Farley did. Two years earlier Bat Masterson

had raised a big purse for a prizefight, over ten thousand dollars. He was going to hold the fight in Texas, one of the few states still straddling the line on whether or not big-time boxing was legal.

The governor of Texas had put the kibosh on the fight, out-lawing the sport and threatening to call out the Texas Rangers. At the last minute the fight had to be moved to El Paso, south of the border. There was big money in it—bigger than robbing a string of banks or holding up Wells, Fargo.

"Thought you'd like it," Sherm said, eager now. "We won't be hurting anyone. The governor might get his feelings riled some, but by the time he finds out, it will be all over."

"You really think you can hide something that big?" Farley asked. In truth, he was awed. O'Dell had changed. He used to be a petty swindler and bandit. Farley had not realized O'Dell had any genius when it came to crime. And this was not crime, per se, like shooting someone or stealing them blind. This was just bending some strange rules.

"This Willie Crush might have as many as *fifty thousand* people showing up for the crash. That's a lot of people. Seems to me a lot of hanky-panky can be hid behind that many people."

Farley reached for his brandy—Blanche supplied nothing but the best, from her late husband's cellar—and downed it.

Sherm might get away with it, Farley mused. In its way, O'Dell's plan was perfect. Why, he'd even have excursion trains to bring the spectators in. It *was* genius, except that

Farley's admiration was quickly turning into stomach-biting acid. This was what O'Dell had in mind all the time. This is why he needed to own a marshal.

The way the law worked, Farley might not be strung up, but as the marshal who had sworn to uphold the laws of the State of Texas—and the United States—he might be in for a long stretch behind bars. Farley'd been locked up often enough for being drunk to know he didn't like it.

"Sounds risky to me."

"Nothing to it, really. Fact is, there wasn't any need for you to know, except that now I need you to show Clive around Crush, to reassure him everything is sweet. Fact is, as far as the general public goes, it might be better if you just go on tending your business and pretending you don't know your hind end from your elbow, if you catch my drift."

"Seems to me that would be mighty tough to do, with all that pounding and building going on. What about those newspaper fellows who will be coming to Crush? They aren't that stupid, to pretend a big arena isn't there."

"That's a problem, all right. When the big day comes, those I haven't bought off won't catch on until too late. Until then I want you to chase any suspicious characters out of town. After all, you're the marshal."

"Come on, Sherm. What we have in Crush is a boomtown in the making. Already the tinhorns and the cardsharpers are showing up, as well as the calico queens. Did you know a Madame Hortense has been nosing around, looking to set up a house?"

"Madame Hortense? Tall woman, black hair down to

her bustle, heh, heh, and a set of gams like a plowhorse, but nice? That the one?"

"The same."

"She used to operate out of Dallas, before they went real Baptist. Her and me should get along. If you should see her before my visit, offer her a job running our girls. That ought to do it."

"What about this visit? I thought you were going to stay away until the big day and leave running the town to me."

"Well, it's like this, Farley. A man's gotta play sometime, and I sent down two fine women. You'll like one of them, a redhead. Put me in mind of Lottie, in her younger days...."

Farley had no reply to that. There couldn't be another Lottie, not for him.

"Besides, I need to talk to Clive some, and bring down those two deputies I promised you."

"Wait a minute. You threatened me with two deputies of *your* choosing."

"That's right. The two guys you met at the jail house a while back. Men I can trust."

"Bad Lungs and Weasel Face?"

"Heh, heh. I don't think they'd take kindly to that. You might get away with it, though. Heh, heh, wish I'd thought of that."

"So I'm stuck with them. What happens if I need some real help to keep the peace?"

"Weasel Face isn't half bad with a six-shooter, when it comes down to it. Bad Lungs, heh, heh, now, he doesn't like anyone. They'll do."

"*And* keep an eye on me."

"That's about right. And they might help you chase any strait-laced folks away. Those kind we don't need in Crush. Face it, until the day of the train crash, there's no reason for any fellows from the papers to come snooping around, or any proper folks."

"That brings me to another point. When am I going to get the jail? Keeping men locked up in the back of the saloon is getting mighty distracting."

"Bet it discourages the rowdies, eh?"

"Some. But Crush is getting big. I need a place to keep lawbreakers. And Silas said he has to have your go-ahead first."

"I'll write him a note. I needed that arena work done first, to make it look good for Clive Gorman. From what you say, we have enough to show him. Here." Sherm thrust a scribbled piece of paper into Farley's hand. "That ought to do it. Now, I want to hear good things from Clive, you understand?"

"Better'n you think, Sherm. Your prize fight isn't quite set, and you're still angling."

"Could be, but you mess it up, and it's your head. I'll be riding over in a day or so. You have things straight so far?"

"Should I bow and say, yus, marster boss, sir?"

"Come on Farley. Remember what I told you, that if things go well, there's a big bonus in this for you? Might be enough for you to make a fresh start."

"That's my part of this week's take?" Farley asked, staring at the small pile of cash and coins Sherm was pushing over to him.

"Yes. You got any objections?"

"Lots, but it doesn't seem to do me any good. Guess I'll be riding along. Dant's is as good a place to drink as any. See you later this week—unless I get lucky."

Sherm slapped Farley on the back, hard. "Don't push me, Dant. You're already lucky."

Later, back at the saloon in the early-morning hours, when a bullet zinged by Farley's head from out of nowhere, missing by a quarter of an inch, Farley thought maybe O'Dell was right.

But that was the last thought he remembered having for the night. That, and the fact that if he got drunk enough, squinted some, and closed his ears, that new girl Clara did remind him some of Lōttie.

Chapter Four

"Just because I let you stay here one night, ain't no reason I gotta rent you a room for another night," the hotel clerk told Amelia. "Not unless the marshal says it's all right, and I can't say he will, can't say he won't. I don't know that he cottons to your type of woman."

"My type of woman, indeed. We'll just see about that," Amelia harrumphed. "You tell me where I can find this Farley Dant, and I will give that man a piece of my mind."

The lizardlike little man shook his head. "Ain't a piece of mind Farley's used to dealing with when it comes to wimmen." He gave a high-pitched cackle. "Don't know that he can be found, least not till later."

Amelia turned on her heel and flounced away, high-topped, practical shoes clanking down on the boardwalk in front of the ... establishment? The boardwalk ended abruptly, giving on to the rutted street she remembered from the previous night.

She would catch up with Farley Dant, before that officious room clerk put her out on the street, bag and baggage. No marshal was about to tell her, as the clerk was trying to, that she could not rent a room in a public facility.

And she would track him down, with or without help from that sycophant cackling over his ledgers. Crush was not that big. Dant should be back today, and he couldn't be that hard to spot. She knew the type, big, greasy, and swaggering. He probably wore one of those broad-brimmed hats, with his six-guns hanging on his hip below a fat belly.

Yes, she knew his type, all right.

His mode of attire might be different from that of the men she had met before—he was likely unwashed, as so many of them out here were—but underneath, he would be of the same breed. Arrogant.

She was already convinced he was one of those men who patted you on the back and told you to adjourn to the company of the ladies after dinner—so *he* could have his brandy and cigar and man's talk.

Amelia had known small-time officials in the city back East. She had known men who thought they were the greatest thing since the steam engine, and she disliked them intensely.

Back home, that kind had always called her "young lady"—a term she despised—in that voice they used to talk to backward children. Or lately they pointedly called her "miss," in a manner that implied she was deficient because she could not catch a man. Who wanted them?

Here they used "little lady." Well, there was nothing little or stupid about her, as Dant would soon find out. She was not about to be railroaded away from her project.

Soon all the men would have to sit up and take notice. She was going to expose Dant—and all the men like him.

Tracking Farley and confronting him would give her great satisfaction, Amelia decided. He probably believed all this hero ballyhoo himself, and she was just the woman to take him down a peg or two. Just because he shot someone, that didn't make him brave or noble in Amelia's eyes. She loved besting men of his ilk. And she knew how to shoot, too.

She had her portable Hawk-Eye with her, loaded with continuous-roll film. She had a small notebook in her valise. Let Dant get nasty. She would get back at him.

Armed with this resolve, she stiffened her spine and marched out into the heat of the morning. She squinted into the Texas sun.

The skies here were big, she granted them that, so big that they dwarfed the construction going up, dwarfed the ramshackle collection of buildings and tents that had the audacity to say, "In a few weeks we're going to be a genuine town."

She looked up Broadway to the left. Strange, but the tone of the town changed north of where she stood. Even the framed-in railroad platform and official post office looked uninspired. Any small town in America could have those. These days it was the sinful tarnish of bordellos and wide-open saloons that was hard to find.

Hammers clanged. They drowned out the sound of her stomach rumbling. She had missed dinner the night before.

Next door to where she had lodged, Dant's Saloon and Dance Hall was doing a muted, early-morning business. A few old codgers were ambling over for an eye-opening snort.

As the saloon swamper swooshed a big broom past the bat-wing doors, raising clouds, she saw a bullet gleaming in the dust. "Howdy, ma'am," the swamper said, staring at her with tortured eyes, as if he did not believe what he was seeing.

That stopped her. She eyed the gleaming pellet of metal. She smelled the stale beer and old sweat, the sorry odors. She wrinkled her nose at the debris left over from the previous night.

The swamper was a classic type, Amelia thought. Dissipated. His face showed the ravages of drink. It had been a strong, masculine face, once. That morning it was whiskery and blank.

This was true grit, more what she was after. She wondered how close she'd get with her camera. The light seemed bright enough. It would not be a traditional shot, but she found something revealing in it: the swamper, the cloud of dust, the gleam of sunlight reflected from the bullet he now held in his hand as he stared at it with awe. The photograph might not come out, but she would try.

"Could you hold it right there?" she asked the swamper. "I will take your picture." He should be happy with that.

She fumbled with the Hawk-Eye. The swamper probably had never seen anything like it. He reeked. Through the lens she saw the man more clearly—it did not seem so much like brazen staring, looking through the camera's eye.

My, he was tall and lean, not an ounce of spare fat on him. Hard to tell what his face was like when he wasn't suffering from a bout with the bottle. She surveyed him, trying to decide which angle to shoot from. His jawline was firm and nicely formed. His shoulders were broad. He was not scarecrow-thin, only toned and muscular.

Her eyes were drawn to the cut of the man's trousers, the kind made of denim with brass fittings riveted right on them. Below the trousers the man wore clean boots, but not the fancy, tooled-leather kind she had seen on cowpunching dandies, boots that made a man look like a strutting peacock.

But it was the Levi's jeans she could not seem to take her eyes away from—only because they were a different kind of garb, she assured herself.

They were rather revealing, she realized as her finger toyed with the shutter release. The faded cloth hugged this man's calves and thighs and emphasized his narrow hips. More shocking, the worn part was a bit more worn right in the front by the fly, which was clearly outlined.

"I don't know what you're up to," the man finally drawled, as if waking from sleep, "but I don't want you pointing that thing at me. Now skedaddle, and leave me in peace."

"But I want to immortalize you," Amelia protested. "This could be an excellent photograph. 'The Wages of Sin'? No, that doesn't have the right ring to it. I wonder if anyone has ever done a picture called 'The Morning After.' The bullet in your hand, there, could you raise it up to your face a little ... that's good, lean against the broom a bit more, there, there, hold it."

Farley slammed the broom to the ground. His brain wasn't churning around quite right yet, but he was damned if some strange hoity-toity woman was going to examine him from head to foot.

Farley had staggered down to check on his dim memories of the previous night. He picked up the broom while he was at it. He wasn't proud about work around here. And he found what he was looking for, a .44-caliber slug. Was someone after him—or was it just another jasper having a wild night? Thing was, Sam had customers check their guns at the door.

The bullet felt real enough in his fingers, though his nerves were still numb. The woman in front of him, well, if she was real, she was trouble. Feisty-looking, bold. Must be a mirage. The woman he woke up with had red hair, as far from natural as he was from sober, and smeared eyes. Couldn't tell what this woman's eyes were like, with that strange contraption in front of them.

He would deal with this later—after a few more hours of sleep, Farley decided. He was going to use the entrance next door, rather than the saloon, to get to his own room. He wanted to avoid Clara. Coward, he told himself.

Farley yelled, directing his whiskey-graveled voice toward the bar, "Gus, finish sweeping. And get rid of the little lady out here. Don't know who she is. Find out, will you?"

He turned and stumbled right by Amelia, heading for the door she had recently exited. He probably did chores for the immoral rooming house as well, Amelia thought.

She was left holding her camera. Strange man. At first something about him had appealed to her—the way mongrel dogs did—but he was unpardonably rude, throwing that broom down just when she was about to snap his photograph. He would deal with her later, indeed! She did not intend to take any guff from some swamper, or the man he called Gus.

So she, too, turned on her heel and stormed down the street, heading south. She'd be back to Dant's, after she had a decent breakfast. She would let them know she was a force to be reckoned with. Well, what could she expect from men who worked for that Farley Dant?

Dant was a man who ran a house of ill repute, as well as a saloon, Amelia reminded herself. The previous night made that clear. She never imagined that men and women coupling would dare make such strange noises, especially when they knew how thin the walls were, giving the tenant in the next room a veritable symphony of subhuman grunts and groans.

Now, the men she would have expected it from, but some of the noises she heard came from women. Disgusting. They sounded like they were enjoying themselves immensely. They laughed between the grunts. Well, maybe it was all right for them, but Amelia certainly couldn't imagine herself jollying up to a man in bed. Perish the thought.

Still, long after the noises had stopped, she had lain awake, strangely uneasy. She had felt empty, as if she were missing out on something.

She would put it out of her mind. She always got slightly restless when she was about to embark on a photographic project, and this was her greatest one, the one that would make her famous. And she would not let Farley Dant stop her.

But she needed to eat, to keep her strength up. She saw

a gentleman heading down Broadway. He wore a slick, soot-colored suit and a bowler hat. He might be from civilization. He had a grizzled appearance but a pleasant countenance. "My good sir," she called out, attracting his attention, "could you tell me if there is a place to eat around here?"

"They told me there's a café place here. Sam's, they called it. Would you care to have me escort you?"

Amelia hesitated. Propriety? What did she care? He looked pleasant enough—and not from around here, either. "I accept your kind offer. I am new in town myself. Miss Amelia Bloomer McCoy."

"My name's Clive Gorman," he said, taking her arm. "McCoy ... McCoy ... you wouldn't happen to have an uncle, would you?"

"Many of them, back East," she said. "May I inquire of whom you are thinking?"

They were strolling like proper folks. His glossy black eyes wavered, looking right and left rather than right at her. His smile, under a bushy mustache, was encouraging, though. He finally said, "Sylvester McCoy, the sporting man?"

"Oh! Uncle Sylvester. What a coincidence that you know him. He was the one to encourage me to travel to this ... this place. He suggested that Crush would make a thrilling photographic subject, and I am beginning to believe he was right."

They chatted all the way to Sam's Café. It was a storefront place featuring "down-home cooking."

"It depends what kind of home you come from," Amelia commented, taking out her handkerchief and wiping dried gravy, the previous night's, and crusted eggs yolks, that morning's, from the oilcloth covering the table.

Clive nodded and tried to catch the eye of the tawdry woman shouting to the kitchen enclave, striding, heavy-hipped, back and forth, slapping large plates overfilled with food on the tables. For each man she served—and there were no other women customers besides Amelia in Sam's Café—she had a wink and a leer.

When the woman—her name was Flo—yelled over, "What can I get y'all?" Amelia replied, "two four-and-a-half-minute eggs, toast—of healthy wheat bread, if you have it—and a bracing pot of tea."

Flo's sweaty armpits made half-moons on the calico dress she wore under her gray apron. More beads of sweat jiggled off into the air, a few landed like pearls on Clive's salt-and-pepper mustache as she said, snorting, "Don't know what chickens you know, but Sam's eggs come one way—fried, with taters and steak. And coffee, lessen you want a snort instead—and that's bring yer own. Take it or leave it."

So Amelia took it and managed to eat heartily as she talked with Clive Gorman. It was nice to run across someone from home. Knowing her Uncle Sylvester, she could imagine that Clive's business had more to do with sporting than with banking or journalism, but it was nice to have a friend and ally.

Before they parted, Amelia said, "Mr. Gorman, I'm sure I can count on you if I have any trouble? A single woman on her own in a strange town and all...."

Clive's black eyes ricocheted around before landing on

Amelia's smiling face. Sylvester was a big bettor—even had some money in this project, if it came off. His niece had to be all right, strange but all right.

"Of course. Just call on me."

Chapter Five

"Not now, Clarence," Farley said, waving the room clerk away, heading for the stairs to his room. "Had a rough night. Anyone's looking, tell 'em I'm out of town till noon."

"But we got trouble ... women trouble," Clarence protested.

Over his shoulder Farley called, "Don't I know it! There's a redhead, a new sister of joy, who knows I'm not out of town. Anything comes up, let Gus take care of things for now. Don't call me unless there's a shooting—and then, don't call me unless it's fatal."

"Yes, Marshal Dant." The room clerk sighed, adjusting his green-tinted visor. "But you might be sorry."

I already am. The sorriest thing to come down the trail, Farley thought. Why he had carried on with Clara the night before, he couldn't fathom. Or why he had had a snootful of red-eye when he swore he was going to cut down. He had been, too, except on the days he went to West.

It had to be the load of horse manure O'Dell had laid on him yesterday, Farley realized. He would have to sober up some today. He had a town to run, and that was getting more complicated every day.

Besides, he had to figure how to save himself from a long stretch in the pokey, from what O'Dell had told him. There wasn't any way O'Dell could pull off that fight without somebody ending up behind bars, and Farley strongly suspected that that someone was him.

He could run out, he thought, but for how long? How far? Sure as the honorable judge was a crook, O'Dell would have a wanted poster out on Farley before he was one hour out of Crush. And running went against Farley's grain. He just flat out couldn't do it anymore.

Wearily he made it up to Room 12, legs heavier than two-by-fours. Without taking his boots off, he stretched out on the narrow bed and slept. It was an uneasy sleep, fitful.

He dreamed of redheads—that Clara had been a hellcat, hotter than a smoking pistol—and heavyweight boxers. All the fighters were pounding him directly in the temple.

Next door, in Room 13, Amelia was fuming. Dant would not be back until noon, she had been told, and she was not about to hang around in some saloon waiting for him. Although, she considered, it might not be a bad idea to catch up with Evelyn and Clara, the women she'd met on the train the day before.

Did shady ladies, she wondered, start work before the sun went down? Perhaps she ought to find out. Yes, that would be putting her time to good use. First, though, she needed a bath. And that meant an interchange with that detestable little man downstairs; Clarence, she'd overheard his name was. She would need him to fetch hot water for her.

Suddenly Clarence seemed the perfect target for her pent-up anger. Just let him try to tell her there wasn't any bathwater in this place!

Within the hour Amelia was soaking in the galvanized tub at the end of the second-floor hall, even though, as Clarence protested, "It weren't a Saturday no-ways."

Naked up to her ears in water that was more lukewarm than hot, Amelia began to feel better. She scrubbed vigorously and washed her long hair. She arched her back and stretched her long legs.

She was just beginning to relax when she heard the door being pushed open forcefully. She had latched it. The latch pulled off the wall as easily as a knife slicing butter.

The door groaned open on its hinges.

Amelia crossed her hands over her exposed breasts. She never! A tall man was standing not two feet from the tub, buck naked except for the towel around his middle. Amelia saw a wound that started on his left thigh and continued farther up, along his side above his waist.

"How dare you barge in on me?" she asked, finally raising her gaze to look at the man's face. It was the same lout she had encountered earlier, the swamper. Had he followed her? Was he thinking of—amorously pursuing her? God forbid.

He shrugged. He acted as if breaking in on a woman who was completely disrobed was not a serious breach of etiquette. "Pardon. Thought you'd be through by now, from what old Clarence said."

"Out—get out or I will scream!"

"I'm getting," he said, drawing the towel closer, "but I wish *you* would get out before the water turns ice cold."

He left—and left her wondering just what he'd meant by that. What had he expected? To be welcomed into her bath? Did he think—could he think—she was one of those fallen women? What difference did it make if her bathwater got cold, unless he was going to use it *after* her?

She finished quickly, dried herself until her skin was raw, and fled to her room, shouting back into the hall, "I'm through!"

Farley would have given more thought to the woman in the bathtub—the same one he had seen earlier, and she *was* trouble—but by the time he got cleaned up, shaved, and dressed, Clive Gorman was waiting to see him.

"Mr. Gorman's at the saloon," Clarence whined. "One of those slick types, wears a hat looks about like a fat cow pie ... but, Marshal, don't go yet. There's this woman, the one made me fetch bathwater, and it ain't a Saturday no-ways, she stayed here last night, on account of you weren't here, and I told her I couldn't give her a room, and then she jest falls over like, some woman thing they do, and ..."

Farley paused at the door. He believed in delegating

55

unpleasantness. "Tell her we haven't got a room for her. Train leaves at three."

"But, Marshal Dant, I told you, I've been telling her," Clarence said.

"Tell her again." Farley did not care for Clarence, who was one of O'Dell's people. "I want her out of this hotel and out of town. You handle it. You're the front-desk clerk."

All around, this had not been Clarence's day—he said he was clerk and that's final, not towel boy or errand boy, and the marshal better get that straight. Now Clarence had orders to handle the strange Eastern lady. That made the day just a little brighter for Farley.

Dant's Saloon and Dance Hall was a large, rectangular room, with a long bar running from front to back along one wall. The rails were pot metal rather than brass, but then, so was Dant's badge, the badge he'd left in Clara's room, along with his gun.

Farley had sent a grumbling Clarence over to retrieve them. No way he was going to tangle with that redheaded hellion again today, maybe ever.

Dant surveyed his domain: several green felt gaming tables, including one for high-stakes poker; a tinny piano; and other tables varnished to a high sheen. These tables his barkeep Gus called whiskey-tea tables, referring to the girls' usual drink, unless they sneaked in a real one.

The current jail stood out, plunked down in the back of the saloon like an oversize cage. Damned flimsy chicken wire, good enough for a man almost passed out but not for real trouble. One man was locked in there, a leftover from the previous night. Farley'd fine him and set him free. He'd be glad when a proper jail was built. He needed it.

Only Snaggletooth Alice was downstairs working the tea routine; it was just past high noon. This time of day, customers tended not to be too fussy about looks.

The man standing against the bar rail in the bowler must be Gorman, Farley thought. The description matched. He looked like he was from back East but not too straitlaced.

Farley knew how to spot gambling men, shysters, and con men. Their heads and eyes bobbed from side to side, instead of focusing in a straight line. They favored fancy-cut suits that shone in the sun. They talked faster than a New York minute, as if their pitch were running a race with an unseen opponent.

Maybe, just maybe, Farley thought, *I can queer this boxing deal without O'Dell being any the wiser.*

Farley eased up to the bar—Gus was making a show of polishing mugs, wiping the grease off—and said, "Mr. Gorman? I'm Farley Dant, the marshal around here."

Clive bobbed his head around, looked Farley up and down, noted the holstered six-shooter and tin badge. He nodded. "We met. But now you look the part, all right, straighter than a deacon, a hero for the masses. I like the looks of you, Dant, and O'Dell tells me you are *our* man. Pleased to meet ya, Dant, pleased to meet ya *again*. Yes, sir, I've been doing some snooping, got a few questions, and I think I can contact the boys back home, if you know what I mean, and tell them to get rolling for ten days from now."

All this went spinning by Farley's head. He felt sharper, though, than earlier. The bath had helped, even if he got it secondhand, and almost cold. He motioned to Gus for a beer, asked Clive if he'd care for a beer or a shot.

"Glass of my usual," Clive told Gus, contorting his face slightly.

Farley watched as Gus poured from the bottle that held tea so dark, it looked like whiskey. Interesting. Clive wanted everyone to think he was a drinking man, but he wasn't. Smart.

"From what O'Dell said, you're nosing around trying to make up your mind about Crush."

Clive sipped and nodded. "There's a few details my investors back home want cleared up, but that's about right. Off the record, what do you think of the plan?"

Farley had not been expecting this. He said, hedging, "Guess everybody knows what happened with Bat. Same thing could happen here, I figure. Prizefighting isn't exactly legal."

"Lots of things aren't these days," Clive commented, stroking his mustache as he watched Snaggletooth Alice hustle a customer upstairs. "But there's ways around everything, aren't there, Marshal Dant? Even hanging for murder?"

So much for discouraging Gorman. O'Dell told him everything. What now? Just go along with him, I guess, and let the chips fall where they may. But I sure don't like it.
"If you say so. It's your money."

"Not exactly," Clive said, head bobbing. "What I need

from you is, how many people are going to show up? What's the schedule on trains coming into town? September twentieth, right? that's firm, that date, no delays?"

"As far as I know."

"You're the marshal. Tell me, you met this guy Willie Crush? When's he get here? What's his cut? For that matter, what's yours?"

"I thought I was supposed to show you around, show you the sporting area, convince you what a nice town we have here."

"You don't recall last night too well, do you?" Clive Gorman asked, filing the information in the back of his head. "That Evelyn gave me one helluva ride, though I favored the redhead some to start. I know what kind of town you got here, and what kind of man you are. A man with an eye on the main chance, same as the rest of us, right? I just need some figures for the boys back home, and we can go with it, no problem. The arena's all right. These fight fans, what do they care, long as there's lots of action and someone to take their money. And that's where I fit in, arranging that."

"So what do you need from me?"

"Your cut and Willie Crush's payoff, when you two gentlemen collect. That'll about do it."

"That's O'Dell's business. He told me he'd give me a bonus. How much, I don't know. What he's doing to take care of Willie, I don't know."

That seemed to be the answer Clive Gorman wanted to hear. Farley didn't know anything—beyond the basics, that a fight was going to take place. "Smart, aren't you, Marshal? I like that. Yes, you just leave running this show to us, and you take care of the train crash. Yes, indeed, that's the way it ought to be. You'll do just fine. Only one more question."

"Ask away." *Between O'Dell and this sharper, I'm a pawn in the game. I get locked up now on a big one, I'll be an old man by the time I get out. But really, what difference does it make?*

"You have any money you want to invest? Seems only fair that I give you a chance."

"I believe I'll pass, Mr. Gorman."

"Clive, Clive to you, Marshal, seeing as we're friends. Well, then"—Clive polished off his tea—"I'll just thank you for this drink and be on my way. Might stick around tonight, give Clara a whirl...."

As if I'd care, Farley thought. But he sensed Gorman wanted him to, wanted to rub it in, that Clive was another boss, like O'Dell, and could help himself to what he wanted.

"That's fine with me," Farley said. "Thought she might have a little rash, if you know what I mean, but that shouldn't bother you any. Can't think of anyone but you I'd rather have her selling herself to, right, friend?"

Gorman looked at him sharply.

It took a moment, and Clive started to laugh, ho ho ho, and slap Farley on the back so hard, he almost choked as that Easterner—female variety, though she walked like a man right now—strode through the bat-wing doors, looking madder than a wet hen.

Or was that before, when he walked in on her in the tub, that wet-hen look? At the moment, with her nostrils flaring and her high color, the front of her shirtwaist rising and falling rapidly like her heart was beating fast, she looked madder than a whole henhouse put together, going after some poor, unsuspecting rooster.

Farley swiveled his head around and stared at the bottom of his beer mug.

Just short of the bar, Amelia stopped, put her hands on her hips, that contraption dangling from her right wrist, and demanded of Gus, "I want Marshal Farley Dant. Right now. And don't tell me he is not here. The boy at the livery said he's been back since last night."

Clive Gorman's shaggy eyebrows rose about an inch. Farley was still trying to hide. Gus grinned. He liked a woman with spunk. "He's here," Gus admitted.

"Then point him out to me, my good man."

"He's the one got his back to you, ma'am, right in front of your nose."

Farley slunk into himself some, hunching his shoulders. Clarence must have told her—again—that there was no room for her at the inn. And she wasn't taking no for an answer. Farley could feel her sparking eyes hot on his back.

"Mr. Dant!"

Slowly he turned around and straightened his shoulders. He stared right into her eyes. "You're considerably better dressed than last time I saw you, ma'am," he said.

Amelia's mouth fell open.

Farley's mouth fell open some, too, but not for the same reason. Directly in back of Amelia, almost blocked from view, a bronco billie stood hip-shot, gun hand at his side, fingers itching for action.

Chapter Six

Farley pushed Amelia out of the way, spinning her so roughly that she stumbled against the bar before catching her balance. Leaning against the rough planks, the first thing she did was raise the Hawk-Eye and look through it.

"Duck!" Farley shouted to her.

Gorman was quick to respond. He dived for the floor in a shoulder roll and ended up underneath one of the whiskey-tea tables. Amelia's camera clicked once. Gus calmly put down his bar rag and the glass he was polishing, reached for his Colt .45. Amelia's camera clicked again.

Farley's voice went low and calm as he stared into the eyes of the man who was challenging him. Man? A boy, really, with that crazed look about him, that crazed, looking-for-glory look. "Lady, get yourself behind the bar and stay there."

Amelia heard the iron control in Dant's voice, but the last few minutes had been full of surprises, and she intended to make the most of this confusion.

She would get her pictures, and the hell with that swamper, marshal, or whatever he was. She aimed the camera's eye in Farley's direction and snapped the cold, hard expression on his face.

"I'm challenging you to a shoot-out, hero," the young, gun-toting cowboy said, soft and deadly.

"You got no reason," Farley said, still using that calm voice, that voice of authority. "I don't know you and you don't me, but you hand that gun over to Gus there, and I'll buy you a drink."

The man in the jail cage had come to life. "Let me outa here," he yelled. "Put me in a proper jail, where a man's safe."

"You Dant the hero, the big gunslinging marshal, right? I don't want no drink with you, I just want to outdraw you."

Farley knew him then. He'd faced the same man a hundred times or more, it seemed. Barely old enough to shave and wanting to be tough. Probably had a little liquor in him and a big dream of glory.

"There's no call. How about we go outside and talk, you and me? I just bet you're the fastest with that six-shooter, right? I see that new leather holster, and it is fine. I see that shiny new gun, and I just bet you're a fast draw, faster than me."

Farley's brain was racing. Play up to the boy, make him feel good, tell him he was mean and good, and that he didn't have to prove it. Talk him down off that killing edge. . . .

"And I'll prove it."

A snake crawled into Farley's gut and writhed there. He

couldn't talk it out, couldn't prevent it, and that damned lady was snapping away, taking it all in, about to get herself killed or at least shot up.

"Outside, then, so the townsfolk can all see how good you are. There's too many people here."

"I like it here. It's your saloon, right?"

Amelia liked it, loved it. She hated the violence, of course, but her mind was on her photographs, not the danger and cruelty. She got that shot just right, with the cowboy's fuzzy upper lip curled in a sneer.

She backed up, took it all in, the two men. The rustling of her long skirt as she backed away—from close-up to medium distance, to across the room—was the only sound in the saloon, except a slight moan coming from the jail cage.

She'd have Farley now, this easy. Watch him kill this young man just off the ranch—unless he got killed. For some reason this stopped her in mid-shot, made her go still with fear.

Farley's blue eyes showed from slitted lids like cat's-eye marbles, not the clear kind but the type that looked like milky glass. He stepped forward one pace. His hands hung at his sides. All his muscles were tensed and knotted, but he looked as unfeeling and impenetrable as stone.

His challenger was not so practiced.

The cowboy's clumsy, booted feet jerked forward. His itching trigger finger quivered. His eyes were on Dant's, cocksure, yes, only they bulged with the strain.

Eyes, hand, eyes—the eyes told Farley the kid was drawing, told him with a quick, squinty blink.

Farley's hands danced, not nervously, but orchestrated.

Left hand looking slack but bracing for the movement of the right arm. Farley's gun arm struck quicker than a snake's tongue. His pistol danced out of his holster, flashed in the air, and barked out.

The kid's arm was going for his gun, he didn't even have it out in plain view before Farley shot. Farley's bullet caught him in the shoulder, the shoulder of his right arm, his gun arm, and slammed him back into a half circle.

Cordite stung the air. The smell of rotten eggs was strong, as strong as the bluish-black smoke rising from Farley's Colt.

The cowboy's fuzzy upper lip gleamed with sweat. His hat had fallen from his head, a big, broad-brimmed hat of black, a tough man's hat. He sank back on his haunches, looking around him in a daze. His teeth clenched, drawing blood from his thin lips as he tried not to scream or cry out.

He had expected to win.

Failing that, he expected to be dead.

He was in too much pain to be dead, unless hell had tortures like these. Farley leaned over him, knelt down, and took the boy's Colt .44, the new gun, the fancy repeating six-shooter, from the floor.

Farley held it up and twirled the cylinders around, tipping it up and unloading it, letting the six unused bullets fall to the wooden floor. They clunked down, hitting each other uselessly like marbles in a kid's game.

"I don't figure you'll be needing this," Farley said. "It will be a long time until you can handle a gun, and then not as a gunslinger."

The cowboy bit his lip again. He stifled a sob.

"Shoulder will be stiff for the rest of your life"—blood was pouring out the hole in the youth's upper arm—"but it could be worse. You'll never be fast again, not that you were as fast as you thought you were. You'll never make a killer, not unless you want to get killed. And every time you think on it, that pain in your shoulder might remind you that you can be dead easy."

Farley was talking soft and low, rubbing it in, maybe, but hurting with the cowboy, too, pleading that he understand how it was, how it would always be.

Amelia, snapping her pictures, advancing her film, stopped when she saw a tear, not from the injured boy but from Farley's cold blue eyes.

This was not what she expected.

She thought Dant would be glad of the chance to show off, to kill a man for no reason other than to prove he was still faster and better than any newcomer who came up against him. He could have, too. It was not her imagination. She had it on film.

But he had not killed. And he seemed to understand what made the boy go up against him, understand it with pity and compassion, for the boy and for himself.

Suddenly she was ashamed.

"There's a sawbones up the street," Farley told the youngster, the cowboy looked younger and more vulnerable every passing second. "You need some help. I bet that guy there"—Farley pointed to the man who had been locked up overnight and most of that day—"will walk you over there."

"You got no call to make me, Marshal," the rowdy said.

"Unless he stays there locked up, until he can pay the fat fine I was fixing to lay on him."

"I reckon I'd be glad to help him out," the imprisoned man said. Farley rose, walked over, and unlocked the cage. The man staggered out, scratched his crotch and then his head, and gave Farley a puzzled look.

"And then," Farley said, pushing the prisoner forward toward the prone boy, "I'll expect both of you to get out of town before sunset, unless we want the jail cage and the shooting all over again."

"Not for me, Marshal," the now subdued rowdy said. "It's worse'n jail, to watch other men drinking and gambling all night, and me dry as a bone."

Clumsily the newly freed man helped the wounded gunman to his feet. Blood ran down in a puddle on the floor. Together they struggled out into the brilliant sunlight. The young cowboy hung his head. He did not look back.

Clive Gorman crawled out from under the table.

Gus strolled out from behind the bar. He scattered sawdust over the puddle of thickening, darkening blood. When Gus was finished, Farley laid the brand-new Colt in his hand. "You should be able to use an extra, the way this town is growing." Farley tried to smile. It cut a gash in his pale face.

Gus nodded, tossed the weapon on the bar, and went for the broom. The sawdust he swept up was mottled from black to a pinkish-scarlet. He nodded without making any comment. From the way he looked at Farley, levelly and in a manly way, Amelia could tell the bartender admired his boss.

"Quite a show, Marshal Dant, quite a show," Clive Gorman spouted out. "Why, something like that, I would have bet on the cowboy, I sure would. He must've been half your age or less, with that quick look about him."

"I guess it's a good thing for you that you don't bet on gunfights."

"Yes, I bet it is—bet, ho, ho, that's good, isn't it?"

Clive was nervous now, jiggling and nervous, even though he had done the right thing. He had seen enough. He wouldn't take Farley Dant for granted. From the floor, looking up, he had seen Dant's eyes, in that split second before Dant aimed and fired. Dant could have taken that young man out slicker than greased lightning—and he had considered it.

Gus resumed his place behind the long bar. The hum and buzz of the early-afternoon customers swelled in the stifling heat. A last wisp of smoke traveled up, dancing through the dust motes.

Clive looked right and left, avoiding Dant's eyes now, wanting a change of scene, or maybe just a change of mood. He tried for one. "I guess this calls for a drink all around. What will it be, Marshal? And, Gus, whatever the marshal is having, make it the same for me."

"A shot of Squirrel," Dant said. *Let the promoter get a mouthful of that rotgut. He has it coming, just for being here. And me, I can use one myself, my stomach is burning, anyway.*

Clive toasted Dant silently, then, remembering his manners, said, "And you, Miss McCoy? Gus?"

"We don't serve women," Farley snapped.

Amelia was bundling up her camera, coming back from the trance she'd gotten herself in when she was behind a camera. She took out her notebook. She would need names and facts, like the date and the kind of guns the men had used, to go with her pictures.

"A lemonade, please, Mr. Gorman," she said, ignoring Farley's outburst.

"No lemonade here," Gus said, pouring himself a drink, watching Farley.

"You know her?" Farley demanded of Gorman.

Gorman shuffled uncomfortably. Before the shooting, Clive would have said yes, loud and clear, and made it clear that Farley was only a hired hand. Now he hesitated. "She's the niece of a friend back East."

"Well, no offense to her, or to your friend, Mr. Gorman, but we do not want her here, in this saloon or in this town."

They stood there like a tableau, Gus watching, Gorman squirming, Farley glaring, Amelia puffing her breath in and out like an engine working up steam.

"Like it or not, I am here," Amelia stated, her words rising in pitch and volume with every breath. "And I will take a beer. Yes, you heard me, a beer, a refreshing libation for a hot day, thank you, Mr. Gorman."

Farley shrugged, not happily. "Might as well wet your whistle. You have a trip ahead of you."

Gus's arms started moving, and he drew one, sliding the mug across the bar. Amelia reached for it, downed it in one long quaff—Farley'd rarely seen a woman do this, unless her name was Annie Oakley—and slammed it back down. She licked the foam off her lips.

"And now, Mr. Dant—or should I call you Swamper Dant, or just Peeping Tom?—I have a few words for you."

Gorman shuddered. He was usually wise enough to stay away from strong drink. He motioned to Gus for another. She would have to be Sylvester's relative.

Farley leaned back, relaxed, shrewd, powerful, fondling that badge of his. He couldn't help noticing how her hair escaped that tight bun in back, curling in tendrils around her face. It was clean and shiny, with a reddish cast over the dark of it. She was plain, maybe, but when her temper was up, it put some color in her face. A strong face, not pretty but handsome. "What words might those be?"

"I refuse to leave town. This is not the Old West, as you well know. You have no call to chase me out of town."

"I can think of one."

"Just you try it."

Facing down that cowboy had been a sight easier than this. "Obstructing justice. You got right smack in the middle of a gunfight. Gus, toss me the keys to the cage. Either this lady gets her fanny up to the train station, or we lock her up on those charges I just mentioned."

"I never!"

"No, I didn't reckon you did. Maybe Mr. Gorman will escort you to the train station."

Clive's face scrunched up, and he belted back another shot. *Just how close is old Sy to this ... Bloomer woman. Not close, I hope. This is getting a little sticky.*

"No. Mr. Gorman will not. Because I am not going anywhere, do you hear me?"

"The keys, Gus."

Damn, the trouble with a threat was, if they didn't back

down, you were stuck with it, Farley thought. He caught the keys and motioned for Amelia to follow. She went rigid as a board. He grabbed her hand and pulled. For a slender thing she was strong, rooted to the damned floor.

"Either you come along, or I'll drag you bodily."

She did not answer.

Lifting from under her stiff elbows, Farley picked her up and carried her to the cage. Patrons hooted and laughed. "This is a new one on me." A dealer, just coming on duty, chuckled.

Amelia was too surprised to speak. She sputtered, but he carried her like she was a piece of wood. She felt the muscles in his arms straining. She hoped he would get one of those men-things from carrying her, and that it hurt. One of her uncles had gotten that, from lifting a crate of champagne.

Truthfully Amelia could not believe this was happening—and it didn't fully sink in until he had wrestled her inside and closed the door. It was not even a jail. It was an overgrown cage. And the minute she was locked in, Farley turned his back.

As soon as she got her breath back, Amelia shouted, "Mr. Gorman, Mr. Gorman, please get in touch with my uncle for me and tell him that some clown who calls himself a lawman is trying to run me out of town. Tell him to have Governor Roosevelt—*a personal friend of his*—get in touch with the governor of Texas, will you?"

Damn it all, she must be close to Sylvester McCoy— and him a big investor in the upcoming fight, and in with Teddy, too. But it won't do to tangle with Farley.

71

Not me, not after what I saw today. O'Dell, you better be ready to stomp on your boy, because I'm not about to.

Frantic now, Amelia called, "You hear me, Mr. Gorman?"

"I'll see what I can do, but it's the marshal's town."

Farley stared at him. "It is, isn't it?"

"Sure is, and I'm sorry I can't stick around tonight to take you up on that Clara offer. It was Clara, wasn't it, or Evelyn? Evelyn, of course—I wouldn't think of taking your redhead. But I have some pressing business in West."

Farley spat on the ground, close enough, but not too close, to where Clive's shiny patent-leather shoes stood. "Are you sure you don't want me to give you the Crush town tour? Seeing as I'm supposed to be your guide?"

Clive half choked, throwing some cash and coins on the counter. "I've seen enough."

After Clive left, scurrying out like a mouse with a cat on its tail, Farley allowed himself a smile. Ten days to go, O'Dell wasn't about to go scouting for a replacement for him at this stage of the game.

Ten days.

Then, who gave a flying hoot what happened? Farley didn't, really, except he'd rather not go to jail if he had a choice. Still, he now had O'Dell in a bit of a bind, same as O'Dell had him in a noose. And Farley wasn't completely powerless. It was a small, mean feeling, but it was nice to see the fear in Clive, nice to hear the quaking in his voice.

Ten days and it would all be over.

"Let me out of here this instant," Amelia shrieked.

She had lung power; Farley granted her that. And after listening to her bellowing for ten minutes, he realized that if ten minutes was this long, ten days could be one helluva long time.

Chapter Seven

Gorman was in a rush to get to West. He just missed the train heading north, which meant there was no way Amelia, locked up back at the saloon, could have made it.

So Clive hightailed it down to the livery to hire a horse and buggy. He was city-born and -bred, and the closest he'd come to a horse's tail was run-ins with New York's mounted policemen, or betting on the nags.

"Horses are all right to make book on, but I wouldn't want to drive one," he said. "Besides, I don't have time to horse around, ho, ho."

"Can't believe a man could get full-grown and not know how to handle a horse," Johnson, the driver, guffawed.

Clive brushed this off. "What you don't know, young man, is that there's a new day dawning. Mark my words, the horseless carriage is going to be the latest rage."

"Har, har, that'll be the day. Har, har. Uh, Mr. Gorman, my boss says you got to pay now, afore we go."

Annoyed, Gorman reached into the pocket of his shiny

gray suit. He hated paying for *anything* up front, but he figured O'Dell would pay the hire eventually, if everything went according to Clive's plan. This could be the biggest, most heavily bet fight Clive had ever promoted.

And this backwoods Texas judge has no idea what the stakes are, no idea how the telegraph and telephone have modernized the betting industry. Christ, I hope McCoy's niece doesn't put a fly in the ointment. No more sweaty gyms for me, no more punchy contenders with the brains of a cauliflower, no more small-time booking. This is the big one.

"Y'all ready, Mr. Gorman?" the driver asked.

"You bet." Clive grinned, then frowned. He could almost feel that velvet in his hands, and he wasn't about to have some Bloomer take it away from him.

"Give you an extra half eagle if you whip him to a gallop." *And I'll take care of putting the whip to O'Dell ... and let him beat on his boy Dant. Never did trust a man who called himself the law.*

Meanwhile, back at the saloon, the pace of the late afternoon was picking up. Upstairs, the girls were donning their low-cut satin gowns and painting their faces.

Clara was frying her hair with a curling iron. The scorched smell of hair was overwhelming. "Look—just look, Evelyn, I can't make this damned curl stay curled. I bet Farley'll notice."

"Farley, Farley, Farley!" Evelyn hisses. "I'm damned sick of hearing about Farley Dant. He isn't anybody, just a worn-out drifter wears a badge, is all."

"Sour grapes, dear?" Clara smiled, rouging her lips with a color that contrasted sharply with her brash red hair.

"Hardly," Evelyn said. "After all, you didn't get paid for last night. Besides, the judge is coming all the way to Crush to see me. He promised. A judge is more important than a marshal any day, especially when the judge is the one who really runs the town *and* the marshal."

Clara continued to smile smugly, but it was a strain on her mouth. "I don't know what your judge looks like, but I bet he isn't lean and mean like Farley. That man is a tiger."

"And I thought he was the town drunk."

"He is not! He's a hero, like Wyatt Earp, Bat Masterson, and them lawmen. If I ever see my old madam again, do I have a story for her! Thing was, what she told me about Bat, he was just a customer. Now, Farley, I think he's in love with me."

"I bet," Evelyn said dryly, giving her blond hair a final flip. Before leaving the room, she jammed a perfume-soaked handkerchief down her bosom. Men liked that, and it drowned out the smell of the ones who only took a bath once a month or so.

Neither woman had heard about the female prisoner downstairs. It wouldn't have meant much, anyway. Women in their profession were always getting locked up, and it was a fine, and behave yourself and work for the man or madam with the power from now on and don't mess with his or her operation.

Clara had been lying around moaning and mooning about the marshal all day. "Oh, I think I have found him, the one for me. He's strong and manly. You wouldn't believe it."

"I didn't—not when he fell on the stairs," Evelyn

snapped, staring with malevolent green eyes at Clara. Dant had not given Evelyn a second look.

But Evelyn had other fish to fry. The shrewder of the two, she sought out the other working girls—"With no madam around to time our work, how do they figure out how much we owe the house?"—and found out how much of her earnings she could keep to herself.

Earning extra on the side, which the management didn't know about, was very much on her mind. She liked not having a madam around to tell her what to do. Dealing with men was easier. And she planned to accumulate a bundle before the great Crush train crash, and maybe snag a judge in the bargain if she played her cards right.

So the first thing Evelyn saw, when she swept into the saloon—*after* looking over the men for signs of wealth, was the lady in the cage. That crazy lady from the train with the daguerreotype, *and* the detective camera, *and* that funny way of talking like she was a man or something.

Evelyn mistrusted honesty, though she had laughed with Amelia and Clara at the time. What else was there to do on a boring train journey? And she certainly didn't trust a woman who claimed to be doing a man's job.

"Evelyn, Evelyn," Amelia croaked. She had flat run out of voice. Ten minutes of straight screaming had gotten her some attention, all right—none of it helpful—and left her with a voice as raspy as an old hinge.

Pointedly Evelyn turned to Gus at the bar, arcing her hips like a sashaying cow in heat as she turned. "You got a live one for me, Gus? I know I heard some gunfire earlier. What was that all about?"

Gus scowled. "You hear bullets flying, you get yourself

down here for customers. You ought to know that. There's nothing that gets men readier than a gunfight."

Gus suspected he was going to have trouble with this seasoned blond. She had mentioned O'Dell, the honorable judge, a hundred times the previous night. She was too big for her corset, Gus figured.

Evelyn said, simpering, "I was getting my beauty sleep."

"Well, time to catch up. The one over there, with the black beard and a gold belt buckle—looks real to me, not gold-plate—might be talked into something."

Evelyn looked over the prospect. On the train, she had seen that same man, the one whose ears got big when Dant's name was mentioned. He looked clean and like he had some money. New suit and a nice job from the barber on that coal-black beard, but his fingernails were dirty.

Maybe new money—and Evelyn liked that idea. Easy come, easy go with those men, she had found. They liked to throw their cash around. She nodded to Gus and sidled away.

Amelia watched Evelyn get to work. Amelia's spirits sank. Evelyn would not be of any help; her idea of sisterhood was throwing her fellow females to the ground and maybe kicking them for good measure, after she pulled their hair out by the roots.

Amelia wondered, for the umpteenth time in what seemed like as many hours, how long it would be before Clive Gorman rescued her. Amelia hated name-dropping, but she believed, if you had to drop one, *Teddy* was as good as any. That ought to put the fear of God—or at least the governor of Texas, who certainly knew of Roosevelt's reputation—into a small-town lawman.

So when Clara oozed into the saloon, all bubbles and bangles and bosom under an umbrella of sausage curls, Amelia did not shout out. Evelyn had taught her a lesson, and what could she expect from women who sold themselves to the lowest sort of men?

But Clara spotted Amelia and rushed to her side. "Aw, honey," she said, "you didn't tell us you was working the other side of the fence. Small town like this, they got unwritten rules, like, and you got trouble when you try that. You sure don't look the part. But I'll tell you what, I'm real close to the marshal, and maybe I can use my influence."

"Thank you. I would appreciate that kindness." *I'm not about to explain—I don't understand why everybody wants to run me out of town, anyway. Maybe Clara can get me set free, if Uncle Sy and Teddy can't. This is a strange world.*

"Hey, what have we here," drawled a rancher dripping with tooled leather and gold horns, replicas of the longhorn variety. "What's this little lady doing locked up? She don't look no Belle Starr to me." He stared at Amelia but fondled Clara's flank.

A crowd began to gather. Amelia had been sitting on the rough wooden bench; her confines were only four by four, and she had gotten tired of standing. Stray drinkers and gamblers had been laughing at her and tossing comments her way, but they hadn't truly listened to her.

Now, following herd instinct, the men and saloon girls made a semicircle around the so-called jail cell.

The dandy Evelyn was wooing—her hand was straying under the tea table to encourage his interest—also became curious. "I'm going to mosey on over and see this. That's the jail, and all it's fit for is holding a helpless lady. Some town this Dant has going."

Evelyn sipped her tea, lips curled down. She hated to lose a live one—even temporarily. Because she would have to wait on him now, revive his flagging interest. It would cost her time, and *her* time was money. Damn that Eastern suffragette or whatever she was.

Trapped, Amelia listened as questions and off-color offers flew through the cigar- and whiskey- and hops-smelling air faster than a mating jackrabbit.

"That what calico queens look like back East?"

"She's part of a gang, I bet, just don't look the part."

"Where's the marshal? Calling in the federal sheriff? She's a bad one, all right. Just look at that hunk of metal she's carrying."

"Some marshal we got—allowing a weapon on her."

"Bet she hid it under her skirt."

"I would've checked! Yes, ma'am, it would've been a pleasure."

"I think she looks mighty proper, fer a criminal."

"Maybe we ought to have some fun, bust her out of here."

"Hmn. *That's* when Dant will show up, and I hear he's still fast with a gun."

Amelia couldn't stand it. Her head was ringing. She was on exhibit. She was tired. She was thirsty. She was hungry. She needed a chamber pot. She was sick to death of this.

"Stop! Stop! I am not an animal. I am a woman ... a working woman who—"

"Amen."

"Honey, I'll pay the fine myself if'n you're strapped."

"You jest look me up when you get sprung, and you and me can do some business. Always had a hankering for an old-maid schoolteacher of mine, looked something like you."

Amelia saw the faces leering at her, closer and closer, avid, distorted, curious. She whipped her Hawk-Eye into her hand and pointed it at the gawkers out of frustration.

They scattered, all but Clara.

"Dumbest marshal. Locking up a crazy lady with that thing. Bet it's more dangerous than a Peacemaker?"

"Don't look like any gun I ever seen."

Their voices receded. No one was brave enough to stand in front of the pointed camera. Clara started to laugh. She hooted. "That's a newfangled camera, you yellow-bellied varmints!"

The men started to laugh, the quiet, forced laugh of men who have been embarrassed, caught with their pants—or their courage—down. The sound rose and filled the saloon, competing with the chink of chips on betting boards, dealers calling a turn, and general mayhem.

Then, starting at the front entrance and traveling back to the jail cell, a wave of silence rippled through the honkytonk.

Marshal Dant loomed there, gun at his side, a mean look on his face. "I told all of you not to disturb the prisoners."

Shamefaced, men eased back to tables, back to the betting and the drinks and the girls. Clara eyed him greedily, like a starving man looking at a steak dinner, and shook the attention of the rancher who had been pawing her.

"Honey, how about I introduce you to Snaggletooth Alice over there. They say she's the greatest"—the customer's eyes widened at the whispered word—"west of Mississippi."

After handing him over to Alice, Clara took a table by herself. She remembered her ma telling her, years ago, that she was already in the back of the barn when God handed brains around, but she *did* know enough not to rush up to him. She would just sit pretty so he knew she was available—and willing.

Just the same, the table she took was a back one, by the cell. Farley'd have to come back there, she figured. Then, tired from all the heavy thinking, she settled down to wait.

In the first place, Clive Gorman got O'Dell out of Blanche's bed. That might have been a blessing, Sherm admitted, but he was just about through, and leaving unfinished business made Blanche just a little harder to handle.

In the second place, the last thing O'Dell wanted to hear was that Dant was giving trouble, after he had been given direct orders to cozy up to Gorman.

In the third place, O'Dell was ready to cut loose, do some stomping and romping. So, as soon as Clive filled him in on what was happening in Crush, O'Dell said,

"Let's go. I'll show you how I keep my man in line, you can bet your boots."

Clive, who didn't wear boots but patent leather, agreed, bobbing his head this way and that, not looking directly into Sherm's porcine eyes.

"The thing is, should we telegraph Sylvester in New York, ask him about the old maid? It's your head—and mine—if they are close. Which reminds me, you better get the telegraph set up there in Crush. You can't run a scam ... er, a business ... these days without a telegraph. Looks good, though, looks good. And I'll tell you what I'm going to do, set it up, yes, set it up. September twentieth, what a day for a sporting man. And about these excursions, could we, say, get a special Pullman put on, for the fans, not the two-bit fans but the big ones?"

Gorman finally paused to take a breath.

Sherm O'Dell breathed a sigh of relief.

"Slow down there, Clive. Down here in Texas, we take it kind of slow, if you get my drift."

Clive bobbed impatiently. "Well, how about it? What are you going to do? You got the answers? My boys in New York will want to know."

"You got Gentleman Jim Corbett lined up. I can take care of the rest."

"In my pocket, Sherm, in my pocket."

"Then let's get cracking. I've had a hankering to get over to *my* town, anyway."

Chapter Eight

"Really, Marshal Dant, do I need an armed guard to use the ladies' amenities?" The acid in Amelia's voice could have etched through solid pig iron.

Farley motioned with his gun, silent.

Amelia swept past him into one of the upstairs rooms—from the peacock-feather hat tossed on the dressing table, she thought it must be Clara's place of ... employment.

Modern plumbing at Dant's Saloon and Dance Hall was limited; this, at least, would be private. Farley promised.

Amelia had been getting desperate. Had she not been so angry, it would have struck her as funny; a man with a tin badge escorting her, Amelia Bloomer McCoy, daughter of a Bloomer, sister of a Pinkerton, a force to be reckoned with in her own right, to a shady lady's chamber pot.

Under the circumstances it was humiliating.

It was not until she was through that she looked around the room more closely. Bed, washbasin, dressing table. It did not look too different from Room 13, the room Amelia had occupied the previous night.

Farley had walked her up here like a homing pigeon. No doubt he not only ran this house of ill repute, he also frequented it. Detestable ...

"Are you through?"

"Marshal Dant, I am finding it increasingly difficult to be civil to you," Amelia called back through the closed door, and through gritted teeth. "When will you be ready to end this farce?"

"When you are."

"Never!"

She was finished with her pressing business, but she stood on one side of the flimsy barrier. She was in no rush to be locked up again.

As it was, the men and honky-tonk women had stared and smirked when she finally had insisted on the trip upstairs.

"Listen to reason, Miss McCoy. This is no way to behave. Leave town quietly and that'll be the end of it."

Amelia pulled the door open sharply, so that a whoosh of air hit her in the face. She found herself inches from Farley's face. From his breath she could tell he'd had a few, and not good-quality whiskey, either.

Their eyes met.

"You know very well you can't keep me locked up forever. It is a disgrace and an embarrassment, and Mr. Gorman is sure to contact the proper authorities. You will get your comeuppance then."

"What does a lady like you want in a town like this, anyway?" Farley asked. Truly he was puzzled. He would think a woman of her kind—obviously well bred—would be glad to flee Crush.

"It's something a man like you could never understand, but suffice it to say that I have my reasons ... and connections."

"So you keep saying. I'm the marshal, and I say you are up to no good. I don't want you here, and my word is law around here."

"Is it?"

Farley scowled. "This is getting mighty ridiculous. I don't want to see you locked up. You don't want to be locked up—particularly down there, with all those men making eyes at you. I'll pay your train fare myself."

"All this shilly-shallying is getting us nowhere. I refuse to leave Crush. So, now, what are you going to do?"

Farley thought long and hard. She was tougher than most men he had faced down. She was not going to back down. In spite of himself, he admired her. Why was it so important, anyway? Because he had made a stand in front of Gorman? Or because he wanted Amelia to think he was in charge?

What was O'Dell going to say? Who was this Sylvester McCoy they kept talking about? Amelia's uncle—but what else was he? Another promoter like Gorman? A man involved with the big fight?

Could Amelia have been sent here to keep an eye on things? A woman? That could be ... and it got Farley's back up once more. "Come along. A night in the cell, you'll change your mind—and you can pay your own train fare."

Amelia had seen him wavering. For a second she

thought she had a chance. Now it was gone. His jaw muscles clenched with determination. His eyes went hard.

"Tarnation!" she muttered as she plucked up her skirts, held her head high, and marched downstairs and back into her cell without another glance at the marshal.

She sat rigid on the hard wooden bench, staring straight ahead as the activity of the night swirled around her.

"Dant, I could kill you over this," O'Dell said as he swaggered into the saloon and dance hall, followed by a weaving Clive Gorman.

"So you've threatened a time or two," Farley said evenly, turning from his hip-shot stance at the bar.

"Maybe this time I mean it."

"What seems to be the problem, Judge?"

"You know damned well what it is, Dant. I gave you orders"—O'Dell's voice shrilled loudly, so Gus and the others could hear—"to take care of Clive, here. And what do you do? You insult the friend of a friend of his and shoot up *my* saloon for good measure."

"And I thought you needed me," Farley said lazily. "Seems to me you also gave me orders to get rid of journalists and troublemakers and honest folks, Sherm, so I've only been following orders. As far as Gorman is concerned, I offered to give him the town tour. Isn't that right, Clive?"

"Yes, Marshal, I mean, yes, Sherman, he sure did. I'm sure this is just a misunderstanding. Just plain unfortunate that the woman is related to Sylvester. Why, the marshal will do the right thing, I'd bet my pocket watch on it. Isn't that right? The marshal, he sure did treat me all right, then this thing came up, and it's just a mis—"

"Cut the bull," Farley said, watching Clive Gorman squirm with fear. "The situation, as I see it, is that I have been following orders. Get rid of straitlaced folks, you told me. Get rid of strange types snooping around. So, the lady's locked up. By morning she'll be begging me to get on that train."

I know better, Farley thought. *That particular lady will do just what she has her mind made up to do. Still, it doesn't hurt to tell O'Dell that.*

Sherm stroked his third chin, a bad habit of his when he was pondering. "Naw," he decided. "We'll do this *my* way. I got a way worked out. The lady will be happy to leave town, but she'll also be grateful to me for getting her set free. By tomorrow ... why, she might not even want to wait for the train."

Amelia saw them there, conferring. She was not surprised when Farley came by with the key and let her out. She bit her tongue, rather than say thank you. She accepted the introduction to Sherman O'Dell, along with Gorman's fawning nods and bows.

"Just plain unfortunate, a big mistake, and I hope you don't hold it against me or my friend here. The judge rushed right over when he heard how his marshal was treating you. You write to your Uncle Sylvester regular, you tell him that, will you? You tell him that his friend Clive Gorman has been looking after you."

Sherm oozed chivalry. "My dear lady, I hope this has

not colored your opinion of our little town." He leaned in closer to her ear. "You must realize how difficult it is to get civilized lawmen out here."

Farley was out of it, walked right away from Amelia and the others after he released her. He was sitting over with Clara, who looked happier than a pig in a wallow over this turn of events. His face was drawn and he was downing a stiff drink.

Sherm could not let it go. "I'll keep my man Dant in line from now on, you can be assured," he told Amelia. "Why, this place is kind of rough for a lady of your breeding, and that's a fact, but we welcome you, same as we would your uncle."

Amelia detested O'Dell on sight. But by now she had to admit that her judgment was warped. So she accepted O'Dell's apologies, *and* Gorman's groveling, and fled from the saloon.

The piano player was banging away and the girls were circulating, except for Clara over with Farley, and Evelyn, who was displaying a length of ankle and garter-adorned thigh to O'Dell. The gamblers were intent on their games of chance. The drinkers were drinking. The folks were folking.

"You mean you're going to pay me a double eagle to break in on the little lady? And you a judge? Heh, heh, she might like me fine, a lady like that, locked up for so long. You think I need a shave afore I kiss her?"

"I want you the way you are. I bet you haven't had a bath since last month, and you a mechanic, building this town in the heat."

"You got no call to say that. Had a bath last Saturday night, or the one before that for sure. But ladies, maybe they expect a shave. Reckon she'll like me, huh? Should I tell her the judge sent me?"

"Idiot. I'm paying you to keep your mouth shut. You get the key from Clarence, go up to her room, and pretend you're a customer. You tell her all the women who stay here are painted cats, you got that?"

"Judge, I'm not dumb." The construction worker's voice was slurred, giddy with drink and the prospect of cozying up to a woman—any woman. "But if'n she likes me, it won't cost me nothing to go for the whole shebang?"

"She won't like you," Clive said, a little apprehensive. "Sherm, you better tell him he can grab her, slobber her up a little, but that's as far as it goes. A blood relative, after all...."

"You heard the man. Tell you what, I'll raise you a half eagle if you do just like we tell you. If you carry it too far, I put you in jail."

"Aw, Judge, I thought this was just a little funning...."

"Right—as long as you do it my way. You scare her good and then come back here, I'll give you money to buy a real woman."

"I surely will, just like you say...."

* * *

By half an hour past daybreak, Amelia had bought herself a tent and a gun. She purchased both from Sam, who ran the storefront café.

Usually silent—as in Silent Sam—the potbellied cook bellowed, "You want to buy *that?*"

"Yes, I will pay cash for your present accommodations. And I would like to purchase a firearm as well, to ensure my privacy. There are some rough types loose in this town."

Sam wiped his greasy hands on his apron. This was his lucky day. The oiled canvas was worthless. It leaked. Besides, a few bugs any man could get used to, but that little shelter plumb bred them fast and mean.

And this McCoy woman was offering thirty dollars for the raggedy old tent, if Sam could throw in some protection. He had a useless derringer around, which he had taken from a gambler who had passed out in his plate of fried eggs and taters after a three-day poker game. Sam didn't cotton to derringers nohow.

"Gun will cost you extra."

"I will pay it. But I want to be moved in immediately. Here—cash money. Take it. And I will need some assistance to move my daguerreotype and luggage. Hurry, I implore you."

"Well, little lady, I got people will be wanting breakfast, would cost me some money, if'n they had to wait."

"Let them wait, I assure you I will compensate you. Come along now. That's a good man, hurry."

"Bedroll will cost you extra. It's wild, woolly, and full o' fleas, so I'll only charge you a Lincoln skin."

"Mr. Sam. I do not require your bedroll. In fact, please

remove your personal belongings, and don't give me any of your housekeeping items out of the generosity of your heart. The tent and pistol will do nicely. Now hurry, before the whole town wakes up."

Clarence woke up the part of the town that counted when Amelia moved out from the boardinghouse part of Dant's Saloon and Dance Hall.

First off Clarence thought it was good news. He figured she had hired a ride out of town, after what happened last night, with that unkempt fellow mistaking her for a shady lady, sort of accidentally on purpose.

Still, when Clarence poked his head out to see, she was trotting down the street, followed by Silent Sam, who grunted without even a proper howdy for the hotel clerk, and she rushed right past the livery.

Curiouser and curiouser. Clarence loved gossip, and business was slow. He marched himself right out past the boardwalk, even got his snakeskin boots with the pointy toes dusty in the street, to eye her progress.

And damned if that woman didn't plunk herself right into that tent of Sam's, as if they had a thing going. But when she started dumping stuff right out the front flaps, good stuff like Sam's bedroll, Clarence knew something else was going on.

Seemed Crush had a new resident. Clarence couldn't wait to pound on O'Dell's door and share the bad news.

* * *

O'Dell was unhappy.

Gorman was not too pleased.

Dant was caught between grinning and swearing, though he could not have told himself just why.

Amelia was miserable. She had stood her ground, but her new dwelling had fleas, large beetles of an indeterminate variety, and small roaches of the kind the slums back in the city bred.

In fact, Amelia's disgusting residence stunk worse than a saloon and a whorehouse at daybreak. Silent Sam had not been a good housekeeper. Amelia, busy with her photography, was not much better, once she swept and fumigated and purchased new bedding from the emporium.

She was too busy. There was a lot to photograph.

The judge, for one thing. Amelia did not know why, but she sensed something in the man, something evil. So when she went over to Dant's to take the pictures she had promised of Clara and Evelyn, she managed to point her camera at the honorable judge. He smiled his oily smile but did not look pleased.

Far less interesting, from Amelia's viewpoint, was recording the opening of the new jail and post office. Then, too, railroad men were swarming through Crush, checking over the track and the railroad platform.

Willie Crush showed up, and Amelia took his portrait, puffing on his cigar, looking like Gorman's twin with that bowler and those keno-ball eyes rolling around, only cleaner and not so underhanded.

Willie was all puffed up and proud and later told Dant that the lady photographer had to record the crash for history. It would be a momentous event.

The duel of the iron monsters was only five days away now. "Whatever else is going on in Crush," Willie said out of the side of his mouth like he knew about the fight but didn't want to know, "you'd better see that the crash is a spectacular, law-abiding event, you hear?"

Dant, worn out from another night with Clara that drained him and left him hating himself, agreed morosely. "It's my job to protect the citizens. Only maybe you better think about doing some protecting, too. That engineer of yours, Wade Puckins, doesn't seem to think things are fine and dandy."

"Wade's an old worrywart. What could go wrong?" Crush chortled. "Those Baldwin engines are fine, and I got everything planned. You tend to your law, and I'll tend to my railway event, and we'll get along fine."

"I still wish you'd talk to him. Wade and I had a drink or two last night, and he asked me if I'd ever seen a boiler explode. I haven't, and I don't want to."

"Marshal, you leave that to me, you hear? You don't know trains the way I do, mark my words. This is going to be a spectacle you won't forget—and safe as a baby in its mother's arms. Just don't interfere."

Chapter Nine

Victoria Bloomer McCoy was in Colorado wrapping up a case when she received the telegram from her sister Amelia. The case involved a Philadelphia embezzler who had been an avid fan of dime-store novels.

Tracking him was relatively easy, but catching him proved more of a challenge. Feminine wiles caught him off-guard, however, in Denver's most prestigious hotel. Victoria was only three years older than her sister but far more worldly.

Five years out West as an operative had wiped out her Eastern primness. In fact, she had been having an affair of the heart—as opposed to liaisons in the name of business—with Stanley, the man who ran Pinkerton's Denver office. Like her sister, Victoria was tall for a woman but far more solid and womanly.

"I'm glad my baby sister finally decided to show some gumption," Victoria told Stanley, "but her timing is most inopportune. Perhaps I should put her off—here, what do you think of this?"

Stanley read the message. " 'Arrested by Marshal Farley Dant of Crush. Freed by Judge Sherman O'Dell of West, portrait arriving under separate cover. Attacked by unknown assailant. My tent ransacked by same. Fight promoter Clive Gorman here. Sylvester McCoy might be involved. Entire town highly immoral. Crush crash scheduled for twentieth September. Please help. Amelia.'

"Arrested, attacked, and robbed . . . your sister? Living in a tent? What does she do? She isn't in . . . our line of work, is she?"

"Certainly not, Stanley. Last I remember, she was being courted by one of those banking sons, a third son with buck teeth and a nervous stutter. My father was so relieved, until she reared up and refused to marry him. That was a while back, and she has not had a proper suitor since."

It took Stanley a moment to phrase his thoughts delicately. "From what she said, could she, uh, have gone into a line of work your family disapproves of?"

"Heavens, no. Amelia is a Bloomer, more Bloomer than McCoy. She is a suffragette and a photographer, and totally disinterested in men. I fear she will never grow up. She has, um, very high ideals."

"You mean she is a—"

"Yes, I am quite sure of it. Which is what makes this so out of character. I can't imagine why she was arrested . . . and in a place like that . . . her!"

"When the picture she promised arrives, let me look it over. In the meantime it wouldn't hurt to check these names with Pinkerton's list, I suppose. Dant ... I seem to know that name from somewhere."

"Oh, Stanley, I have so been looking forward to our little ... idyll. I hope this does not interfere. And, Stanley"—Victoria leaned over so her ample bosom snuggled into his arm—"should you find my uncle involved in anything, you will suppress the information, won't you? After all, from what you told me, your family also has a black sheep."

"Baaa," Stanley mumbled.

The information Stanley assembled was this: Farley Dant was once a respected lawman who had dropped out of sight until he apprehended and killed bank robber Deadeye Dick in West.

The hirsute bandit had been on Pinkerton's wanted list. An operative, sent to check the dead man's identity, had disappeared. Reportedly the same operative had been seen in New Orleans, flush with cash. Pinkerton's was rather sensitive about this. The company refused to issue the reward money on Deadeye until the situation was checked out.

Sherman O'Dell was another can of worms.

There was no Pinkerton listing for a judge by that name, but a man calling himself Shirley O'Day was wanted for holding up a train. Stanley was quite excited when Amelia's portrait of the judge arrived; it could be the same man. An operative, possibly Victoria, needed to confirm this.

Gorman was well known in boxing and betting circles.

The law—and Pinkerton's—did not like him, but they had never had anything concrete to get him on. It was rumored that Gentleman Jim Corbett owed Gorman on some illegal bets back in New York City, but nobody could prove it.

The strange thing was, what was a fight promoter doing in Crush?

The planned train crash was most interesting, but it had nothing to do with Pinkerton's, except that the old man had suggested it might be worth keeping an eye on. Petty swindlers and possibly bigger fish were sure to be attracted to it.

Sylvester ... well, he was a close blood relative of Victoria's, and if she could keep silent about Stanley's brother—how he regretted talking so much that night—he could certainly disregard that information.

The telegram announcing Victoria's arrival did not go unnoticed. "Here, Marshal, you better have a look at this," the telegraph man said.

Gorman, who haunted the newly built communications office, jumped up from the chair he was growing into, demanding, "That for me? Judge says, telegrams for me, you don't fool with, eh, Marshal? Right? Nothing against you, Farley, and no hard feelings?"

"It's not for you," Farley said listlessly. Damn, he'd be glad when this was over. A few nights running with Clara on his back—or close to it—was enough to make any man listless.

Farley read: " 'Arriving in Crush before crash. Sister Victoria.' "

Afterward, when Amelia received the news—a boy came calling for her at the despicable tent—she suspected it had been tampered with. There were sweat marks on the thin yellow paper. Amelia was glad her sister was discreet.

Farley, for his part, knew this was exactly the sort of thing O'Dell expected him to report, which is why he decided to let it sort of slip his mind.

After all, the way Farley figured, O'Dell had outsmarted himself with Amelia, which is why she was a town fixture by now, snapping away with that combination camera of hers. And, incidentally, causing problems with the law.

Her property had been broken into one night while she was trying her hand at poker, right at Dant's table. She wasn't a bad player, either, Farley had to admit.

She complained bitterly about the lawlessness in Crush, but from what she said, none of her money had been stolen. She claimed some fool had taken her continuous-roll film, though, but whoever the thief was, she had outsmarted him. The film he stole was not yet exposed, and her pictures were already sent out.

Farley had listened, though there wasn't much he could do. Arrest some saddle bum for stealing film? That was ridiculous, even if Farley could catch the man.

In fact, Farley had had more than one run-in with the strange lady. They were always prickly encounters, like coming up against a quilled porcupine, but for some damned reason Farley enjoyed seeing her around, enjoyed trading insults with her. Most of the time.

He couldn't put his finger on it, but she reminded him some of Lottie. Not the way she looked—Amelia was so proper, he wanted to shake her sometimes, always dressed like an old maid with her hair severely pulled back—but in the way she comported herself.

Like Lottie before that grifter stole her pride away, Farley thought. *Smart, but not putting on airs about it. Interested in things, kind to people, but no pushover. She has courage ... even if I can't understand why these pictures are so important to her. And she sure can get hot under the collar. Wonder what this sister of hers is like ...*

But Farley did not have time for idle speculation.

The locomotives were coming to town, under their own steam. More girls were arriving. Just last night O'Dell's friend Madame Hortense had taken over running the girls, taken over the whole upstairs operations of Dant's Saloon and Dance Hall. It was going to cost Farley his percentage, but he didn't care. It might get Clara off his back—or wherever it was she perched whenever she got the chance.

Farley had rival madams tucked away in the new jail, women who refused to work for—or with—O'Dell. It was his job to run them out of town. Orders from Sherm, who believed in free enterprise as long as it was his.

The boardwalk on Broadway was completed now, and Farley's boots made tapping sounds against it as he strode up to the respectable section of town. He could see the gawkers gathered around, and they were not there to see the madams catcalling from the jail house, either.

A shiny, newly painted Baldwin locomotive, followed by

a second beauty with similar diamond stacks, was slowly pulling up in front of the new station.

Workmen put down their tools and hooted and hollered.

Farley spotted Amelia, dressed in a shirtwaist, her hair askew, snapping away. This he could understand. Pictures of these monstrous engines would be a keepsake, something nice to have. Thirty-five tons each, Willie Crush had boasted—and he was right.

One engine, number 999, was painted green with red trim. Number 1001 was all shiny red with green trim. Each monster would pull rolling boxcars arrayed with ads from the Oriental Hotel in Dallas—a lot of Dallas people were expected for the big event—and from the Ringling Brothers Circus.

Without realizing it, Farley had crowded in close to Amelia. Her elbow hit him in the gut.

"Umph."

"Pardon me—oh, it's you."

"Yes, and that *was* my stomach."

"Well, could you please move it? I had the perfect angle on engine number 999 until you came along."

"Why, I just wanted to see the sight. What do you think? You think it's going to be the most wonderful thing that has ever happened in this part of the world, like Willie Crush says?"

"For this part of the world,"—Amelia aimed and focused again—"he might be right. What I don't understand"—snap—"is how they are going to crash without anyone getting killed."

"Wish I knew. Trainmen say they will remove all the

spare pins and loose tools. The men who have volunteered are the most agile trainmen alive—"

"Let's hope they stay that way. I was talking to a Wade Puckins"—snap—"only yesterday, and he expressed some grave reservations."

"Guess we all have them. Look, they're moving them over to the special track. You heard if the regular train is coming through on schedule?"

"I hope so. I'm expecting company."

"I mean the one traveling north, to West."

"Are you implying I am expecting the one traveling south? And just why, might I ask, would you imply—"

"Don't get your dander up. I was just making conversation."

Amelia whirled to him and snapped his picture. "There. I have it. Guilt written all over your face. Have you been reading my telegrams?"

"Miss McCoy, are you judging me?"

Amelia turned her eyes away. Of course, that's exactly what she was doing. And why not, when the man had jailed her, tried to run her out of town, and was himself run by that tub-of-lard judge?

Farley caught her arms and pulled her close, so she had to look in his eyes. She saw the pain there. She had seen it when he'd winged that cowboy he could have killed.

Farley's intensity was embarrassing. "There are things you don't understand," he told her. "Maybe when this is all over, I can tell you. Maybe then you won't look at me like that."

"And why not? That O'Dell owns you. You run a saloon and a whorehouse. You're no kind of man I can respect."

Farley's voice went husky. "By God, you're right, but I can't help it. I didn't plan it this way. I didn't plan any of it and I don't like it, and there's damned little I can do about it."

His grip was painful. Amclia drew away.

It was like having a bad man fall at her feet in confession, though what Dant was confessing to, she could not imagine. She wanted to throw her arms around him and tell him everything would be all right, even if she did not respect him.

But she was in dangerous territory and she knew it.

So instead Amelia said, "I hear the northbound train. You'd better get the women you're running out of town on it. That is the way you operate, isn't it? Whoremaster. . . . ?"

The sudden fury in his face died away, leaving a hollow shell. "I guess it is," he agreed.

And as he turned away a far corner of the boxing arena caught his eye, confirming that what Amelia said was true. He was no longer a man. He was a puppet in O'Dell's game, and soon the strings would be pulled.

Oh, God, I need a drink, Farley thought desperately. But lately even the red-eye could not pull the curtain down on Crush and his job as marshal. Nothing could.

Chapter Ten

Chief Engineer Wade Puckins was still a robust, powerful man with a full head of gray hair. He was missing the last joints of two fingers on his right hand, from his days as a brakeman, when a truculent link and pin took them. He had no regrets; the deformity, as much as his striped hat and red bandana, was a badge of the early days of railroading.

The Missouri, Kansas, and Texas Railroad was Puckins's life. He was a widower, but he mourned the passing of the pioneering days of the railroads far more than the passing of his wife. She had been shrewish and given to headaches.

"When I was a boy and saw my first train, a little spur line west of St. Louis," he used to tell people, "it was love at first sight. Worked at laying rails"—he still had the burly muscles to prove it—"three strokes to the spike, ten spikes to a rail, four hundred rails to a mile."

He would tell new men, with wonder in his voice, "The excitement never leaves you, never."

He had also worked as brakeman—he still shivered when he thought about climbing over swaying boxcars in the freezing snow to set the old-style hand brakes—baggage man, station agent, and fireman, the job that made Tallow Pot seem like a personal nickname.

"But engineer, full engineer, that's a job a man can be proud of." Besides, it *was* nice to sit on the four-dollar-a-day side of the train.

And Puckins was proud, a stickler for details, a brave and dedicated man. He knew every trestle of the Katy, and could recite like a litany the names of railhead towns that were created by the expanding railroad.

Railroading was dangerous business, though—even after the new law was passed in Washington making air brakes and automatic coupling mandatory. The law had come about, Puckins recounted, because ". . . in 1888, the first year those rich stockholders thought to check, two thousand railroaders were killed on the job, and twenty thousand injured."

At Dant's Saloon and Dance Hall, Puckins talked railroad safety to anyone who would listen, sitting for hours over a single mug of beer. Farley Dant listened—and heard the fear behind Puckins's words.

"I tell you, Marshal, something is clutching at my heart like the grave. I've survived one train crash, back in '79, I've seen some others"—here Wade shuddered—"and I tell you, it's a dangerous job. The tracks, trestles, the couplings, the boilers don't get you, the highwaymen will. But what newfangled kind of highwayman is this Willie Crush? Who'd want a train to crash for the fun of it?"

"Why don't you ask him?" Farley said. "He's over there."

"He doesn't look like one of us, does he? He's fat and sassy like the stockholders, making their fortunes out of the sweat of the railroaders like me."

"Well, all I can say is, he doesn't look like any workingman I ever knew," Farley agreed. "That ten-dollar smile and big havana, those flashy clothes ... Wade, you told him about what you think yet?"

"I've been trying, but you know this type, all flash and grin. He isn't listening to me. If the stockholders back in St. Louis like the duel-of-the-iron-monsters idea, he isn't going to listen to an engineer. Not now, when he has them convinced it's good publicity, and he's the big shot behind it. He's not a railroader like the rest of my crew."

"From what you said, I think we're going to have problems. Why don't you try again—I'll send over some drinks on the house."

Wade nodded. "Thanks, Marshal. I will try, though it's about like talking to a boxcar. Well, I guess we each have our own cross to bear. O'Dell back in West?"

"Until tomorrow," Dant said. "He's getting some final papers on the Crush plats, gathering up some salesmen to sell lots."

"Railroad brings a lot of changes to a place, doesn't it?" Wade said, rising reluctantly. "Used to be I thought all of them were good...."

* * *

"Willie, mind if I sit awhile? Dant said he's buying, and I'd like to talk to you." Puckins hated this, but he was driven. "Did I ever tell you, Willie, about how I personally financed a trip to Baldwin's great engine factory in Philadelphia to make some technical suggestions on boiler design?"

"Seems you were running off at the mouth about it, but I had other things to do. Still do."

"Well, all I ever got out of it was a handshake, but they used my ideas, and I'd like to think maybe I saved some fireman's life down the line."

"Real interesting, Wade, but I got things on my mind besides ancient history."

The drinks arrived. Willie was looking around for an excuse to grab his and leave. The only working girl around was Snaggletooth Alice, O'Dell was out of town, and Gorman—Willie related to him like a brother—had not shown up yet.

"All right, let's get to modern history. History in the making, you call it, don't you, Willie?"

"Puckins, the board says this collision is going to be a humdinger, and I say it's going to be a humdinger. What else is there to say?"

"People are going to get killed, that's what. I have a crew of fifteen of the finest men who work the Katy all fired up about this, going along, wanting that bonus ... but I'm chief engineer and I don't like it."

"You don't have to like it. Just follow orders."

"Orders? When it comes to running a train, I thought the engineer gave the orders. I've been telling you, I helped develop the finest engines known to man—and now you are going to destroy them. I have trouble accepting that."

"Slow down there, old man," Willie said, puffing a fresh havana. "Times you came from, sure, a railroad was a railroad. These days there's competition—yes, competition with a capital *C*. We're moving into the twentieth century. Think of it, old man. We want the Katy on everyone's lips—and it will be, because of this here show."

"Some show, Willie," Wade said dourly, sipping his beer. "Either one of those engines could serve a whole territory. Beauties, each one of them, even after some twenty years of use. Now, bam, destroyed for some goddamn show. You haven't seen a boiler explode, the way they used to in the early days . . . and the same thing could happen here. I tell you, I don't like it."

"You don't have to like it," Willie said, blowing a fragrant cloud of smoke at Puckins. "You do what the bosses say. You're the engineer, but they're the men who pay your wages."

"I sent them a wire—"

"I told you not to do that."

"Why? I need to go on record. I don't like it."

"You want us to call in a younger man? You want to quit? You're flapping your jaw all over, scaring the folks. You yellow? You don't understand promotion—that's the real lifeblood of modern times, I tell you. Not equipment, not miles of track, not service, but hoopla. So we destroy two old engines—it will be a spectacle people will remember the rest of their lives."

"I've seen some spectacles men remember, all right. You ever hear about the crash outside K.C. in '89?"

"This is different. This is a *planned* crash. Tickets are selling like crazy. Did I tell you, we even got music coming from some new composer, name of Scott Joplin?"

"Music?"

" 'The Great Crush Collision March.' Folks will notice the Katy, all right—and they're going to know it isn't some old-fashioned outfit, I'll tell you."

"I saw that crash, back in '89. I was there. Killed twenty people, fire all over the place, steel flying through the air like bullets, explosion so loud that it knocked the missus's china right off the shelf ten miles away."

Willie Crush stared his chief engineer straight in the eye. "You got it good, old man, and don't forget it. The Katy takes care of its people—unless they're fired for incompetence."

"Looking after safety isn't incompetence."

"Meddling with this collision, scaring folks, that's incompetent. Now, I want you to keep your mouth shut, old man, or I'll have you fired and replaced. You just do your job, that's all—and without jawing on it."

Willie Crush stood up and changed tables.

Puckins made a big night of it and had a third beer.

The Telegraph office was a small wooden building situated between the new jail and the train station. Clive Gorman spent a lot of time there. In fact, he had gotten friendly with the telegrapher, a man named James.

"Got to shut down now, Mr. Gorman," James said.

"I was expecting that message any minute. How about

I get you something to eat, we play a few hands of cards to pass the time, and wait?"

"I don't play cards. Besides, I have a dinner waitin' on me. First thing in the morning, you check with me. It's already two hours past sundown, an' three hours past closing time."

"I thought we were friends."

"Sure enough, but a silver dollar stretches only so far in a night."

"Here's another."

"Fifteen more minutes is all."

Just then the telegraph started chattering. Gorman's salt-and-pepper mustache wiggled. He had been waiting all day to hear from Sylvester McCoy. Time was growing short.

James, intent on his task, translated the dots and dashes into a message. James liked his job. Morse code was music to his ears, and he liked having the edge on what was going on in town. He was an important man.

The chattering ceased.

Bouncing, nervous, eager, Gorman reached for the message. James held up his hand. "That extra dollar?"

Gorman's grizzled face twisted, but he caught it in time and smoothed it out like an iron had gone over it. Gorman could not afford to make an enemy of James. Swift communications were vital to the betting business.

"Here, my friend," Gorman said, chunking the silver on the counter. James palmed it in midair and released the message.

Though he was eager, Gorman restrained himself and

slipped it in his pocket. Together the two men walked out into the darkened street and parted company.

Crush, after twilight, was pretty dead at this end of town. All the action was down by Dant's. The jail was dimly lit, though, by a lantern that reflected from inside.

The marshal's new headquarters ... But everyone knew that if they were looking for Dant, they would find him easier at the saloon.

Which is where Gorman was headed, after he stopped by his room to read his telegram. O'Dell was pressing him, now that the fight was almost on them, about just who was going up against Gentleman Jim.

But things were a bit more complicated.

Gentleman Jim Corbett had threatened to back out, and without a name boxer the betting was going to go to hell and back, strictly penny-ante stuff.

Gorman had wired Sylvester McCoy. In passing, he had also mentioned his niece, Amelia McCoy, not in an out-and-out lie but suggesting that he—Gorman—was keeping an eye on her.

When he read Sylvester's reply, he was glad he had: "Corbett to arrive nineteenth September. Contender Alf Larson. All bets on. Best to Amelia."

Chapter Eleven

Although Amelia had great faith in her lightweight camera—she had been pleased with how natural the pictures seemed—she also needed traditional photographs taken by the more widely accepted daguerreotype.

So, four days before the crash, she lugged her old-fashioned equipment out of her tent and prepared for a serious day's work. She attacked the project with the grim determination of someone accustomed to indoor plumbing using an outhouse.

She was dressed for business. The skirt of her shirtwaist was getting shabby where it swept the ground. Her hair, as usual, was pulled back. She certainly did not look frivolous or helpless.

"Why, Miss McCoy, you need some help with that?"

The townsfolk had grown used to seeing Amelia around, and she was no longer the target of catcalls—or offers of help—though she suspected she kept the rumor mills going. She turned. For a moment she had trouble placing the man calling her.

"Oh, Mr., uh, Mr. Clute." What was the construction supervisor's first name? Silas, that was it. "What a pleasure to run into you. I could use a little help, thank you. Are you having a day of rest?"

"Just taking a little breather. The town's mostly built. Looks nice, doesn't it? We surely were mighty busy. I heard you got settled right in, and I've seen you some, but not close enough to shout. You like it here?"

"I'm finding it ... quite satisfactory." Amelia thrust the bulky black box into his rawboned hands. He staggered from the weight. She held on to the tripod.

"You take a picture of the station yet? Or the new jail? Solid, that jail house is ... and did you get a gander at the post office and shebang since they've been painted?"

"Yes, they are all very nice, Mr. Clute, and I'm sure I will take many more pictures of them. Right now, though, I need a picture of Dant's Saloon and Dance Hall. And my, isn't that some sort of outdoor entertainment area there, in back?" She knew darned well it was. "Did you build that, too?"

"Well, uh, I built about everything in Crush. That's, uh, nothing. Now Dant's, from what I hear, you find that saloon right interesting."

Amelia looked at him sharply. "It has a certain fascination for the people back East, who have never seen anything quite like it. There—just a little farther now."

Silas Clute huffed and puffed. The large box camera was extremely heavy. It was a wonder a slip of a thing like

Amelia could handle it. This picture taking, Silas thought, was no sort of a job for a lady.

Amelia put her hands up to her eyes, working her fingers so they made a small square peephole to look through. She was framing her picture. If she got Silas to place the camera a little to the left, she had an angle on the saloon that also got in a small corner of the arena and wooden bleachers.

As she plunked the tripod down and unfolded its three sturdy legs so they made a pyramid on the dusty ground, she tried again to get Silas to open up. "Here, that gets everything in. I do declare, that looks like a boxing ring to me. But whoever heard of such a thing in a town like this?"

"I surely don't know, ma'am. I build what they tell me, that's all I know." Silas groaned with effort, making the last few feet. He tried to swing the daguerreotype up. He couldn't. Amelia took one side, and together they wrestled it into place. Amelia screwed it securely to the tripod. She beamed.

"Thank you so much. And now, perhaps you'd like to get in the picture?"

Silas fidgeted nervously. "No, I don't reckon I would. Maybe when you get to the post office or the train station."

"Surely you're not ashamed."

"Why, ma'am, why would you say a thing like that?" Silas said shyly. "Every town needs a saloon. I reckon it's more important than one of them city halls. But I'd best be going."

He edged away. He certainly did not want his picture

taken anywhere near the boxing ring. Maybe when it was all over, he'd admit to being the man who built the arena—in the right company, of course.

Besides, Silas told himself, that danged camera was heavy, and he didn't want to get stuck hauling it again. Why, that was real labor. He'd had his breather. He was ready to get back to his supervising.

Amelia did not notice his departure. She had ducked under the black cloth behind the camera.

She focused on the saloon. Strange that it was just another false-front building, like thousands that had sprouted up in the heyday of the West. No matter what she had just told Silas Clute, it was nothing special. There was nothing to distinguish it but the big sign proclaiming it to belong to Dant—and there was the rub. Amelia knew better.

Ever since she had run into Farley Dant the other day she had been bothered. What had he said? Something about things not being what they seemed? If this saloon and bordello was not Dant's idea of the good life, what was it?

It came back to Judge O'Dell. It had not been difficult for Amelia to figure out the connection, not when it was O'Dell who overrode Farley's orders when she had been locked up. But what hold did O'Dell have on Dant? And why was he using the lawman?

Staring through the impartial eye of the camera, Amelia felt she had the answer right in front of her, but she was too dense to see it. Why had she chosen to put the arena in this particular photograph? What was the link between

115

O'Dell, Farley Dant, the great train crash, and the boxing arena? And where did her own Uncle Sylvester fit in?

She wished Victoria would show up. Her sister was surely more clever at puzzles like these than she was, and she would bring information on the people involved.

Amelia bent over and retrieved a photographic plate from her crowded valise. She slid it into place. In the morning hours nothing much was going on, but the light was excellent. She was about to start the long exposure when a dark shape obscured her shot. It was a man she vaguely recalled seeing before, first on the train, then later in town.

From behind the camera she could see large white teeth and a black beard, then his back as he strode toward the saloon. Damn. She wouldn't mind him in the picture—a human figure always worked wonders for perspective—if she could get him to stand still long enough. The clumsy daguerreotype had severe limitations.

She called across the street to him, "Either stand still and I will get you in my picture, or kindly get yourself out of the way."

He must have heard her. He covered his face with his hands and scurried away. His behavior was strangely furtive. She shrugged and got back to work. But no matter how hard she concentrated, she could not rid herself of the tantalizing feeling that the answer to what troubled her was right in front of her nose.

By midafternoon, when the southbound train got in, Amelia had worked her way up to the jail, which was about a block away from the new train station. Bad Lungs and Weasel Face had agreed to pose for a photograph. "Sure thing," Bad Lungs said, wheezing. "Can you get our deputy badges in so's people will know we're the real law around here?"

Weasel Face added shyly, "Ain't that the truth."

"I will certainly try," Amelia promised.

The two of them posed stiffly outside the jail house door, blinking into the sunlight. Although she was not close enough to capture the expressions on their faces, the slope of Weasel Face's narrow head and the slump of Bad Lungs's shoulders made them both look moronic. The glint of their proudly displayed badges would show up as pure farce, Amelia thought.

She was finding that it was difficult to go back to the old-fashioned camera. In the future, she vowed, she would carry her continuous-roll camera as well. It was quick and so much easier. Even a child could handle it.

Amelia recalled that she had learned about the lightweight new Hawk-Eye through Victoria. Pinkerton's was extremely innovative, and they used them. Agents these days carried cameras to photograph the criminals they caught—dead or alive. They used identifying numbers hung around the criminal's neck to aid in identification.

A new term had been coined for these photographs: mug shots, rumored to have come from Pinkerton himself, when he was going through his picture gallery and declared of one pock-faced robber with a face that would make a bulldog look pretty, "With a mug like that, only his mother could love him."

Victoria had written to Amelia about an armed burglar

she had shot in the line of duty, out in Cripple Creek, Colorado. After the fellow was dead, a bullet through his heart, Victoria had to tag him with the number and prop him up in order to take his picture. The photograph positively linked him with a bank holdup back in Chicago.

The man, her letter stated, had rigor mortis and was unwieldy, but her new Pinkerton-issue camera took only seconds to use. Victoria had said the camera ushered in the modern age of law enforcement and detective work.

Amelia had been impressed. She wondered if the same camera could be used for more artistic purposes. She had sent away for her Hawk-Eye that same week. If cost five dollars. She felt a sense of freedom and purpose when she worked with the instrument; she was convinced she was pioneering a new art form.

The trouble was, many journals derided the new, popularized "snapshots" as lacking in quality. However, Uncle Sylvester had a friend at *Colliers* who promised to give the newfangled snapshots a try, to see how they reproduced. Uncle Sylvester seemed to have friends everywhere, not all of them shifty-eyed types like Clive Gorman, whom Amelia had come to mistrust.

Amelia's musings were cut short by the long, loud blast of the train whistle. The passenger and freight train now stopped in Crush on a regular schedule, unlike when Amelia had arrived with a short whistle stop in a place that was barely more than a cotton field.

The stream of passengers departing the train had also become swollen. It was as if the fledgling town was being force-fed, fattened to the bursting point.

After finishing her exposure—Bad Lungs chuckled with

a death rattle and asked when he could have his photograph—Amelia surfaced from her work and looked up the street.

Even at a distance Amelia recognized several working girls from their dresses and posture as they embarked. A few dandies sported fashions from back East. It seemed incongruous to see spats and bowler derbies side by side with boots and ten-gallon hats. The atmosphere was definitely like that of a carnival.

Scanning the crowd, Amelia did not see Dant. Probably back at the saloon getting drunk with Clara, she thought.

Amelia's eye was caught by a buxom woman moving with determination through the crowd. She was tall and dressed in a businesslike suit that hugged her wasplike waist and emphasized her ample hips. She carried her own valise, which was not heavy. She obviously knew how to travel. There was an air of authority about her.

Her hair, a shade lighter than Amelia's, was fashionably swept up from a face partially covered with a saucy little hat and veil. In spite of that, her eyes were piercing and her nose distinctive.

It had been a few years; it took Amelia a few minutes to recognize her older sister.

"Victoria! Victoria!" Amelia shouted. "Over here."

The woman gave an imperious look around. She swiveled her head, looking toward Amelia but missing nothing of the throng and commotion. Amelia was a photographer; Victoria had what some wags were beginning to call a photographic memory. She was always on the job, a Pinkerton through and through, and proud of it.

Amelia stepped from behind her camera and rushed up

the street into her sister's arms, leaving the smirking deputies behind. Through the veiled hat Victoria pecked the air beside Amelia's cheek. Then she took her sister by the shoulders and held her back for a long critical look.

Finally she shook her head sadly from side to side. "Little sister, how long is it going to take you to learn you'll catch more flies with honey than with vinegar?"

Amelia was suddenly aware of her shabby clothes and the sooty streak across her face. Her unkempt hair was no longer neatly pulled back. Sweat darkened her shirtwaist under the arms. Her hands were stained from photographic chemicals. She had been working hard all day.

Worse, she had forgotten how small and awkward her older sister used to make her feel when they were growing up. The four-year age difference was enough to make Victoria the leader, socially and professionally. Amelia had forgotten that although she truly admired Victoria, the admiration did not flow two ways. Amelia still had the childish desire to show Victoria that she herself was not a ninny.

"Well, you are just going to stand there?" Victoria demanded.

"Your telegram brought me all this way. Let's adjourn to a hotel and get to work. And, Amelia, now that you are fully grown and on your own, there are a few things I simply must talk to you about."

Amelia turned back to the equipment she had left by the jail. She started to pack up her camera without replying. Soon enough, she would have to let Victoria know that there was no real hotel in town. The deputies, sensing

Amelia might ask their help, retreated inside. "To guard them dangerous prisoners," Weasel told the ladies.

Victoria tapped her foot on the dusty ground, staring at the new station, at the stone jail, the post office and telegraph station, across at the trestles and extra set of tracks for the crash, and finally down Broadway toward Dant's. She seemed to be searching for something or someone.

"I'm ready, if you can carry the tripod for me," Amelia announced. "My place is down the street—we'll go there first."

Victoria surveyed the situation for a fraction of a second more, spotted a tall man with a badge striding toward the jail, and let out a shrill, long whistle. It caught Farley's attention—and the attention of every living soul in the area.

"I say, my good man—you, with the badge," Victoria called out firmly, "would you be so kind as to help my sister and me to her lodgings? Your deputies disappeared, but of course I can tell you wouldn't run from ladies in distress. I've heard such wonderful things about the sheriffs in Texas."

"Marshal, ma'am," Farley said, correcting her.

"Yes, well, I can see your reputation is well deserved," Victoria said with a smile. "Come along, then, Amelia, give the gentleman your camera and tell him where you live so we can be off."

Chapter Twelve

"Amelia, I've stayed in tents before, but this is ridiculous. Just look at you. Look at this mess. I should send you back to New York right now," Victoria said, squashing a bug under her well-shod foot.

"But Victoria, as I recall, you were the one who told me that conditions in the West were primitive. This is what was available to me. It's a very serviceable tent. There's plenty of room for an extra bedroll, and it's very convenient to Sam's Café."

Almost speechless, Victoria stood in the midst of Amelia's shabby abode muttering about Denver and San Francisco and some man named Stanley of whom Amelia had never heard. Finally, unable to pace in the confines of the tent, she sat gingerly on Amelia's bedroll.

"I agree it's no place," Amelia said, "but I needed someplace, and believe me, it's this or the bordello. And if a respectable woman stays in one of them, someone is sure to think you're a Jezebel."

"There are worse things to be mistaken for," Victoria pointed out acidly. "Like an old maid."

Amelia ignored the barb. "Besides," she said, defending herself, "you yourself warned me not to expect luxuries when there was a job to be done. Remember, you urged me to get out on my own, and the consequences be damned. And unless you just traveled down here to criticize me, there's a job to be done. Something wicked is going on here."

"So I saw," Victoria replied cattily. "If I didn't have an *amour* waiting for me, I could become interested in Marshal Dant myself."

"So I noticed," Amelia replied, equally cattily. "You were playing up to him like a two-bit whore, and he fell for it. He likes your type."

"Why, Amelia! If I didn't know any better, I'd think you were jealous."

"I could never be interested in a man like that," Amelia said hotly.

Victoria's eyebrows raised. "Indeed? And just why is your face turning beet-red?"

The two women faced each other, hostility thick in the air. Ancient rivalries surfaced in their minds. They were both strong-willed women—and with a Bloomer for a mother, neither had ever believed that little girls were sugar and spice and everything nice.

Then, as they glared at each other, each remembering the fights they had had, fights that would have put rowdy brothers to shame, Victoria's lips began to twitch. Amelia's pursed mouth widened out in a grin that threatened to split her face in two. Together they began to laugh.

"Just like old times—" Victoria began.

"Remember old Dudley Mudgette?" Amelia cut in. "How I hated you over him, and then, finally, neither of us wanted him? What a time we had getting rid of that pantywaist!"

"Ho, yes. And Father was absolutely livid at both of us for letting 'that railroad fortune get away.' Father never did get Dudley's name right."

"Mother defended us, though. Remember that speech she made, about the new breed of woman who didn't need to hide behind trousers? Who could go out and make their own fortunes?"

"Brave words," Victoria recalled. "But I thought you were a goner when Father pushed that third son of a third son on you. Banking, wasn't he?"

"I escaped," Amelia said, "but it wasn't easy. At least you chose a profession that is respected in some circles—"

"Not in Father's."

"He doesn't admit it, but I've heard him talking about his daughter the Pinkerton. He respects you. It's me he doesn't understand."

"Well, really, Amelia, a woman photographer is an odd lot."

"The pictures I've taken here will change that. They are truly good documents."

"Spare me, Amelia. No matter how good they are, unless you start getting recognition, it doesn't count. However, I believe I can be of some help to you."

"Help? I thought you specialized in criticism."

"The duty and prerogative of an older sister. Besides, I know far more about the ways of the West than you do.

And, I should add, the ways of men. You must at least pretend to respect them. There is nothing wrong with the advice I have given you over the years, only in the way you have followed it."

"Well, dear Victoria, you must admit I never spent a night in jail—or got robbed—until I sought my fortune out West, as you so often advised me to do."

"I never claimed there would not be perils—I must tell you about the close call I had in Deadwood—but you have to admit that it is not as dull as back home."

This time Amelia stomped a bug emphatically. It crunched beneath her foot. "No," she agreed, "not dull."

"You have regrets, then? You'd rather be stagnating under Father's roof?"

"Certainly not! I think I am on to a story here that will make my reputation as a photographer, and that is worth the hardship and humiliation I have suffered. However, I haven't been able to figure out just what the real story is."

"But I'm sure the persons you telegraphed about have something to do with it. Particularly that judge you mentioned. What is he calling himself? O'Dell?"

"Yes," Amelia said, "Sherman O'Dell."

"Well, let me tell you what I think," Victoria began.

Amelia plunked herself down beside her older sister and listened. They discussed the people involved in the town of Crush, and what Victoria—and Pinkerton's—suspected about them. The sun was down by the time they finished talking and planning their next moves. Amelia lit a kerosene lantern, but it attracted more bugs.

There were many points they bickered about, as was

their habit, but one thing on which they both agreed: Together they were going to get to the bottom of what was going on in Crush—before it was too late.

Over at the saloon, Farley was trying to drink and keep sober at the same time. It was rough going, especially with Clara by his side, closer than a fly on stink. Being around Clara always put him deep in a slough of despondency that triggered an even deeper thirst.

Farley was relieved when the new madam, Hortense of the long black hair and heart to match, came over and ordered, "Clara, hustle your bustle over to some paying customers, or the boss is going to be mighty unhappy."

"I am sitting with the boss," Clara said, simpering, and patting her garish hair with a lacquered nail.

"Honey," Madame Hortense said with a drawl, "I've worked with some plumb dumb ones in my day, but you are truly exceptional. Now, unless you want your job to go to one of the new girls streaming into town, get moving— and smile pretty at the judge while you do."

"Farley," Clara whined.

"You heard the woman," Dant said. "She's running this operation, her and O'Dell. Do what she says."

Clara huffed away.

Farley stared down at his empty shot glass. The whiskey tasted like hell. O'Dell was over at the bar, in deep conversation with Gorman. Gamblers crowded the gaming tables. The bar was packed, and Gus was moving so fast that his arms looked like windmills in a gale. Wade Puckins was sitting at a corner with his lone beer, surrounded by members of his crew. Willie Crush was absent tonight.

Only a few days and it'll all be over, Farley thought. *I said I wasn't goin' to do it, but maybe if I tie on a good drunk, it will all be over by the time I sober up.*

Somehow, though, as Puckins caught his eye, that did not cheer him considerably. So it was out of habit that he ordered another shot and a beer from the barmaid, who now patrolled the tables. Dant's Saloon and Dance Hall was becoming a sophisticated place.

His order was delivered just as Victoria and Amelia marched purposefully through the bat-wing doors. Men turned around to stare. Farley himself closed one eye so he could focus better. The appearance of the older one with the hourglass figure came as no surprise, but seeing Amelia in a feminine, curve-hugging dress with her hair fashionably coiffed did.

Madame Hortense stiffened and looked pointedly at the judge, but O'Dell did not respond. He was whispering to Gorman, "Better if Dant stayed pie-eyed until this is over, so he don't get it in mind to play straight lawman, don't you reckon?"

Unable to get a clue from O'Dell on how to treat the interlopers, Hortense strode over to the two sisters, glaring. "We don't allow no competition around here. Either you work for me or you get yourselves out the door."

"We will just see about that," Victoria said. Then, turning to her sister, she asked, "Could you point out Sherman O'Dell to me."

"Over there," Amelia said, ignoring Madame Hortense,

"sitting beside Clive Gorman, the friend of Uncle Sy's I told you about."

"It looks like we have come to the right place, Amelia. Would you care to make introductions for me?"

The madam's mouth was agape. She recovered and informed them that she would personally escort them over to see the judge—and then they would just see what happened.

"That will not be necessary," Victoria said.

"Honey, I'm not letting the likes of you two out of my sight until the boss tells me what I'm supposed to do with you. No way are you two going to go messing with my side of this business."

"Hey, you girls new around here?" a railroader asked, looking them over from head to foot. "Madame Hortense, you might make a customer of me yet. I want the tall drink of water." He shook his head. "Seems to me I seen the other one before, only she didn't look like this."

Amelia started to explain that neither she nor her sister were for sale, but Victoria swept by the man without comment, her head high. Amelia finally followed her example.

Other customers had paused from their drinking and gambling. The McCoy sisters, together, were a stunning pair, far outclassing any women in these parts. Gorman, recognizing Amelia, cursed under his breath. O'Dell followed suit, quickly replacing his sour look with a smile that oozed false cordiality.

"Ah, ladies, what can I do for you this fine evening?" O'Dell said.

Amelia said, "I wanted to introduce my sister. Victoria

Bloomer McCoy, Judge Sherman O'Dell and his friend, Mr. Clive Gorman."

There was a flurry of handshaking, more suitable to a parlor than to a saloon. Hortense, hovering nearby, was clearly puzzled. "Judge, what am I supposed to do about these two?"

O'Dell hastily replied, "Madam, go tend to your own flock. These little ladies are nieces to one of Clive's friends back in New York. Isn't that right, Clive?"

"Yes, indeed," Clive declared. "Why, just last night your Uncle Sylvester said to say a big howdy for him."

Hortense left, muttering to herself. She hated women she could not control—and those she had under her power she had no respect for. She didn't much like men, either, when it came down to it. Her range of emotions, which ran all the way from mild contempt to downright hatred, made her an efficient madam.

Victoria, relieved at the older woman's departure, beamed a smile at the men in front of her. "I have heard what a charming judge was involved in this town. And, of course, Mr. Gorman, it is always a pleasure to meet a friend of Uncle Sylvester's."

O'Dell warmed slightly at the flattery. This one was not like the lady photographer, though Sherm had to admit that Amelia didn't look too bad tonight herself. "And what may I do for you? A drink, perhaps? Unless you don't drink—I don't want to offend you."

"A brandy would be fine," Victoria said smoothly. "Amelia?"

"Yes, that would suit me as well."

"Gus, two brandies—from my private stock, none of that rotgut."

But once the drinks were in the hands of the McCoy sisters—and by God they knew how to put them back—the conversation flagged until Victoria started flirting shamelessly with O'Dell again. Evelyn, who had just serviced her tenth customer of the night, watched with horror; she still had half a notion she could cozy up to the judge.

"Surely a man of your caliber, Sherm, is wasted in a backwater town like this," Victoria said breathlessly.

Sherm puffed up like a toad at mating season. "Miss McCoy, West is my town, I own it, but you're right. It is just a steppingstone to bigger and better things. With Crush, now, I've been talked into helping out a friend, for this railroad extravaganza, but afterward, I've been thinking, a man like me could go further in life."

Amelia choked on her drink.

Victoria hid a yawn behind a graceful hand but recovered. She noted every wrinkle and line and chin of O'Dell's. Gorman she didn't bother with. He was a petty gambler and prizefight promoter, but Pinkerton's had no doubts about his identity.

Sherm, though, was so buried under that layer of suet, Victoria needed some way to match him up with a much younger train holdup man who had called himself Shirley O'Day. In her own mind she had no doubt that he was the same man, but how could she prove it?

Three brandies later she was still mulling over the problem as her younger sister gave her little nudges and sideways looks that said it was time to leave.

The truth was, Amelia was falling into a thoroughly

strange mood as she glanced toward the back table and saw Farley sinking lower and lower into his misery.

As of midnight—and that hour was fast approaching—there were only three days to go until the duel of the iron monsters. Three days until the excursion trains descended, bringing upward of fifty thousand people to Crush. Three days until whatever was going to happen because of that prizefight arena.

And Farley was hiding in a bottle while O'Dell and Gorman smirked, saying that many old lawmen were nothing but old drunks whose days of glory were long past.

Chapter Thirteen

The McCoy sisters handled their liquor well. They came from a drinking family on their father's side, but it was tempered with iron control from the Bloomer side of the family tree. Or so they told themselves. Still, by the time they got out of Dant's, they were feeling no pain.

Arm in arm, they sashayed through the night singing "Ta-ra-ra boom-de-ay" at the tops of their lungs. It was a lyric that had been popularized by the English music-hall star Lottie Collins several years ago and had just made its way across the Atlantic.

In the distance they heard an answering yodel, which struck them both as hilarious. After they got over their giggling fit Victoria said, "At least you have cheered up. Earlier, I'd never seen such a long face."

"You would have seen a longer one if you'd taken your eyes off the fat toad and looked at the marshal," Amelia said. "He was crying in his beer—until his head hit the table."

"Weak, weak creature," Victoria clucked.

"Ta-ra-ra—Oh, Victoria! I know he is weak, but something about him breaks my heart!"

"A drinking man like our McCoy uncles, and Father as well. I'm convinced O'Dell is a crook, and Gorman too. They are using Marshal Dant, but how I do go on. You don't care, do you? You said yourself you could never have any feelings for a man of his ilk. Maybe he is nothing but a broken-down lawman and deserves what he gets."

Amelia stopped and stood stock-still, suddenly serious. "Oh, no. There is something more to Farley, something brave and honest. I am convinced of it."

"How can you tell? Wasn't Gus, the bartender, mopping him off the floor before we left?"

"For once, shut your mouth, Victoria. I refuse to listen. Don't you see that it's the drink and O'Dell's control over him, not the man?"

"It comes down to the same thing, unless you are going to do something about it," Victoria said needling.

They were almost at the tent now. The chill of the September night had cleared their heads. "*We* are going to do something about it," Amelia said, just as a flickering light showing through a hole in the tent riveted her attention. She grabbed Victoria and pulled her into a shadow.

Victoria's training took over. She fell into a crouching position as she reached under her skirt for the derringer she carried in her garter. "Get behind me," she whispered to Amelia.

They heard a rustling from inside the tent. One tent flap was drawn back slightly from where the intruder had broken in. Amelia saw red. She had already been robbed once. She was ready to storm in without warning. She was not about to lose her latest photographs to some thief. "Do something!" she hissed.

Victoria edged closer, but away from the entrance. Whoever was inside wasn't being cautious—and he would find Victoria's papers, as well as Amelia's work. Slowly Victoria placed her face against the ground and lifted the canvas for a better view. With her unarmed hand she motioned for her younger sister to stay back.

"How many?" Amelia whispered.

"One, but he has a Colt," Victoria reported tensely.

Inside, the shuffling stopped abruptly. The man had heard some living thing. With luck he might think it was a rat, but they couldn't count on it.

"What do we do now?"

"Shh. I'm thinking."

"My pictures. He's after my pictures. Do something!"

"Sing! Run ten yards back and sing," Victoria said. "I'll catch him off-guard as he sneaks out."

"But—"

"Go!"

Amelia scurried back ten paces and opened her mouth. A squeak emerged. She tried again. Tremulously she began. "Ta-ra-ra boom—"

Boom!

The derringer's retort shattered the air. The man's gun bounced off the dirt. He went flying to the ground with a loud wail, holding his bloodied hand. The thick, acrid odor of cordite hung in the night air.

"Jump him!" Victoria shouted.

The ruffian started to roll over, trying to get on his feet

and make his escape, but he was spooked and in pain. Amelia looked from the stoop-shouldered thief—she couldn't make out his face—to the starry skies, to Victoria.

Then, with a whoofing cry, she leapt. Her body caught him off-balance and crashed him back to the ground. She straddled him, skirt billowing up far above her ankles, her hands at his throat.

She stared down into his dull, dark eyes.

He wheezed, "Let me go. I didn't do nothing."

"Thief! I know you now. I took your picture today. Bad Lungs! And you a deputy!"

Victoria tugged at his jacket, darkening now with the blood from his injured hand. A soiled pillow slip came tumbling out. Inside were photographs, exposed photographic plates, and film. More damaging, as far as Victoria was concerned, were the files from her current Pinkerton work.

"I think we'll have to finish the job on him," Victoria said flatly, "deputy or no deputy. Did Farley Dant set him up for this?"

"Didn't take nothing worth nothing—them's just paper and stuff," Bad Lungs protested.

"Don't be a jackass," Amelia said, breathing hard from the effort of holding Bad Lungs down. "This rapscallion happens to be O'Dell's man."

"Amelia, no matter whose man he is, we have to kill him. He's been through my papers." Victoria moved closer and placed the barrel of her ladylike pistol against his forehead. She averted her face. "This is the part I hate," she said, cocking the trigger.

The man's eyes rolled up, white in terror. A stream of spittle escaped his lips.

"Oh, for pity's sake, let him go!" Amelia said.

"Are you crazy? That information—"

"The man's a dullard. He can't read, Victoria. Today, when he was giving me the information about his photograph, he made an *X* for his name. Ohhhhh—"

The brief, single click of the derringer being disarmed was the loudest sound Bad Lungs thought he'd ever heard. He was sorrier than he'd ever been in a plumb sorry life. If the judge or Weasel found out about this, he'd never live it down. Maybe it would've been better if the woman had shot him. Bested by two women and—

"Victoria, can I get off this piece of manure now? He wouldn't tell us anything we don't already know and—ugh."

"Shh. I'm thinking. Amelia, if you are going to pursue this line of work, you have to get used to a little bloodshed."

"Blood!" Amelia replied, highly indignant. "This yellow-bellied cretin has wet himself."

Victoria shuddered. Some sacrifices were going too far, even in the line of duty. Although it was Amelia straddling him rather than herself, Victoria had loaned Amelia one of her best gowns.

"Get off him, quickly! Do let him go, sister," she said. More softly she added, "Stanley loved that dress."

Bad Lungs slunk away, holding his injured hand over his darkening trousers. Getting shot up was one thing, but this shamed him something terrible, and mere women the cause of it. His slow brain was trying to figure how he could get out of town by sunrise without running into anyone he knew.

"As you can see, there are times when my job isn't all glamour," Victoria said as she prepared to bed down. The sisters had straightened up the tent, which had been in disarray. It didn't look any worse than it had when Victoria first saw it. The theft had not disturbed the bugs.

"If I may be so bold as to point this out, I was the one pinning him down when it happened," Amelia said. "And you might be through for the night, dear sister, but I still have a chore to take care of."

"Amelia, there's not much night left. Whatever can you be thinking of doing at this ungodly hour?"

"Just a little something that crossed my mind. There is no way to prove what I think about Farley Dant is true unless I sober him up. And I haven't got much time."

Victoria held her hands over her head, which was beginning to throb. If O'Dell's special stock of brandy could do this, she'd hate to think of what the rotgut did. "Now?" she asked plaintively.

"I *can* handle this myself," Amelia said.

Wearily Victoria said, "Whether I like it or not, we are in this together."

"I'm so glad you see it my way," Amelia purred sweetly.

Determined to have the last word, Victoria added tartly, "But you have to realize that shooting a man is far easier than reforming him."

Gus's eyes widened in surprise. "Isn't it past your bedtime, ladies?"

Dant's was as close to deserted as it ever was these days. A poker game was going on. Snaggletooth Alice, who hadn't had much luck earlier, was waiting for a truly desperate man. The other girls had given up. O'Dell was upstairs, snoring next to Evelyn. The railroaders had left for the Katy sleeping car where they bunked. Gorman was also asleep, dreaming of world-class bets.

"We need a little favor, Gus," Amelia said.

Gus shifted on his sore feet, and his eyes slipped away from Amelia's. "Can't rightly say I'm able to oblige. The judge said to make you welcome if you came in, but that's all."

"Nobody has to know about this little favor but the three of us," Victoria said, batting her eyelashes at him.

"I'll handle this," Amelia said. "This is not the time to shilly-shally around. Gus, you are a friend of Marshal Dant's, aren't you?"

Gus was uncomfortable under Amelia's level, direct gaze. "He was a great lawman, Miss McCoy, one of the best. Why, he cleaned up this whole part of the country when he brought in the Slades."

"And the liquor brought him down, didn't it, Gus? Surely you've seen enough from your side of the bar to know how that changes a man."

"Don't you go turning Carry Nation on me. Drinking is just part of life. I served you two women myself—"

"The point I am trying to make is that unless someone sobers Farley Dant up, he's nothing but O'Dell's dupe."

"Miss McCoy," Gus said earnestly, "ain't nobody ever sobered up anyone unless they was ready to sober up."

The emerald in Amelia's eyes flashed. "Gus, I am not

a gambling woman, but I'd be willing to bet Farley is ready to sober up—with a little help from his friends, that is."

Gus scratched his head. "Dant was drunker than a coon when Clara dragged him up to bed. I just don't see how—"

"Help us get him out of here," Victoria said, "and the two of us will worry about the rest."

"Bring the body, and the mind and heart will follow," Amelia declared piously.

Gus had been puzzling over a few things during the last week, like O'Dell being so pleased with the way Farley'd been slopping up the red-eye. Why this was so, Gus hadn't figured, but he thought it was a shame. With a grin he murmured, "O'Dell isn't going to like this one cotton-picking bit. What do you think I can do to get Farley into your hands without anybody yapping about it?"

He bent close as Amelia's words blew softly in his ear. When she was finished, Gus said, "It just might work, but I'll take you up on that bet, from pure horse sense."

"A five-dollar gold piece?" Amelia asked.

"Make that a double eagle instead of a half," Victoria said firmly. "There's two of us, and our mother is a Bloomer."

Gus didn't want to run into Madame Hortense or awaken any of the sleeping girls. He'd been in the business long enough to have some sympathy for the soiled doves. There were some rough ones, all right, but a woman who made her living on her back had a right to rest it now and then.

So he trudged up the stairs on quiet feet and tiptoed down the hall to Clara's room. He let himself in, thinking about what a fool he was. A man was liable to get himself shot sneaking into an armed man's room. He only hoped Farley'd slept it off enough to listen to sense—before shooting.

And, by God, out of pure reflex Farley reached for his six-shooter the minute Gus nudged him. But Gus grabbed his hand and said hoarsely, "Marshal, it's me, Gus. Come with me. We got trouble."

"Let O'Dell's deputies handle it," Farley said, slurring, then rolled over. Clara stirred. Damn.

"Farley, it's the ladies, those McCoy sisters. They're in big trouble."

Farley rolled over, back in Gus's direction. The gun he held limply in his hand was pointed toward the ceiling. "Oh, Lord, let Bad Lungs and Weasel Face handle it."

"Can't," Gus implored. "It's Bad Lungs that done it. You'd better go quick, before the other bad'n shows up. Those ladies are in danger."

Farley's eyes fluttered, but his brain was far behind, moving sluggishly. Crossing his fingers behind his back, Gus said, "Amelia's in trouble. She needs you."

Amelia's name triggered Farley into action. He swung off the bed.

Clara sighed sleepily. "Farley, honey . . ."

"Law business," Farley growled at her.

"Shh, Dant," Gus pleaded as Clara started to snore again. "Don't wake her up with your stomping and snorting. Come easy. This is O'Dell's doing, the trouble those sisters are in, and we don't want anyone knowing about it except us."

Farley swore under his breath and stumbled down the stairs after Gus. Since he had passed out in his clothes, he was already dressed.

He was groggy, half pie-eyed, and miserable. If he'd just had a little more to drink, he would be safe in the arms of Morpheus right now, dead to the world, instead of traipsing after Gus, trying to be some hero to a woman who had the greatest contempt for him, he thought.

Before leaving the saloon, he tightened his holster and secured his six-shooter. He was halfway through the door when Gus rushed after him and tapped him on the shoulder.

"What is it now?" Farley asked sullenly. "I thought I had to hurry."

"Oh, there's going to be trouble, all right, but it'll wait a New York minute. Terrible trouble. You'll see," Gus said vaguely.

The barkeep's kindly face was distorted, as if he knew something he was busting to tell but couldn't. "But, Marshal, maybe you ought to belly up to the bar first, before you face it. A man shouldn't have to face what you're going to face with a hollow leg, eh?"

Chapter Fourteen

Farley could feel the generous shot of whiskey Gus had given him burning its way down his gullet to his belly. Strange that Gus was usually the one who tried to slow him down, leastways this time of night. Farley wondered just what he was going to have to face.

His reasoning powers were none too sharp, but Farley figured that if it was a life-and-death situation, Gus would have been pushing him out the door or offering to come along, instead of setting him up with a healthy shot. "For medicinal purposes only, and don't you forget it."

No, if either of the women were dead or dying or under attack right now, Gus would not have kept him at the saloon for a spare second. Chances were, from what Gus hinted, that one of the deputies had strong-armed Amelia—or maybe worse.

If either Bad Lungs or Weasel Face had raped Amelia, Farley was prepared to kill him. But something besides revenge was tugging at him.

Farley, who had not prayed for anything since Lottie ran off with Thaddeus Beauchamp, found himself praying that Amelia was all right, undamaged in both mind and body.

He'd seen what a man could do to a woman, breaking her spirit the way a trainer breaks a horse, until nothing strong and free was left in her. He couldn't bear to have that happen to Amelia. He wasn't sure he understood her, but he didn't want to see her spirit broken.

Lord, you and I haven't been friends for some time now. ... I never have had much liking for those church people wailing on Sundays and raising hell on the sly the other six days of the week, but me and you go back a ways.

Sure, I figured you turned your back on me, and maybe you had your reasons, with me being no good to anyone, much less myself, but I could be different.

I don't know why, but you took the best and brightest thing I ever had in my life when you took Lottie, and I evened the score on that one, and lived through it, too ... and then along with the helluva mess I'm in right now, you put another spunky lady right smack in my path....

Please, let her be all right.

Farley looked up into the broad expanse of predawn sky. He saw a bright star wink at him through the clotted clouds. It was a friendly wink, not a son-of-a-bitch wink. Maybe it was just the booze, but he felt like something that had been frozen in him harder than packed Colorado mountain snow was beginning to shift and thaw.

* * *

"Oh, Lord, you can't do this to me!" Farley said through clenched teeth. He was bound at the wrists and ankles with rope, trussed like a Christmas turkey, a prisoner of two determined women.

"Quiet, Marshal, or I shall have to gag you," Amelia said evenly. "Go back to sleep, and in a few hours things will be better."

"Sleep! You're crazy, woman, I'm dying—and that hack your sister gave me on the side of the head didn't help any. God, I need a drink."

"Yes, I expect you do," Amelia said. "Silent Sam's Café will be open shortly, and I've taught the man to brew a very bracing cup of tea. Tea with honey ... I'm told it is very therapeutic for a man suffering the effects of strong drink."

"I think I'd like a cup myself," Victoria said.

"Only thing that will help me now is my gun," Farley said. "I'll shoot myself."

"Perhaps you will think of that *before* you pick up your next drink, Marshal Dant."

Farley groaned. He'd be spitting mad, except his mouth was too dry to work up any spit. When he got hold of Gus, he was going to choke him with his bare hands. And the McCoy sisters? What he'd like to do to them was meaner than a passel of snakes in a barrel.

When he had arrived at their tent, they had caught him off-guard, using their soft words and lies to lure him inside. At first he was relieved that neither of them had been hurt, but that was before Amelia told him that they were going to sober him up, whether he liked it or not.

He didn't.

The thought of it was so fearsome, he must have gotten

wild, raving and pounding his fists into each other. The next thing he knew, the two of them were trying to hold him down. And when *that* didn't work, the older one, Victoria, had very efficiently conked him on the side of the head with her ivory-handled derringer. He remembered seeing stars before the world went black. Those stars were giving him son-of-a-bitch winks.

Now he had a worse hangover than ten end-of-the-trail cowboys put together, and a knot on his skull to boot, and both his body and brain were screaming for relief. He was sweating and shaking and shivering, and Amelia was offering him tea.

He rolled himself into a ball and closed his eyes. He must have dozed off, though he could hear them jabbering in the background, unless it was part of his nightmare.

"Amelia, ever since I met Farley, I thought there was something familiar about him, as if I had perhaps seen him once. You know I have a remarkable memory for faces."

Amelia stiffened, afraid of what she was going to hear, but curiosity got the better of her. "Is he ... wanted somewhere?"

"No. I can't imagine anyone wanting him right now. But remember that job I wrote you about, in Cripple Creek?"

"Yes, when you first used your Hawk-Eye."

"That's the one," Victoria said. "I was only there two days, and that was the first man I ever killed. I was quite unprofessional and upset."

"What does that have to do with Farley?"

"I think he was in the mining camp running some tables for a shady lady there, only he looked different. I never would have made the connection, until now. You must admit, Marshal Dant looks better asleep than awake."

Amelia eyed her sister with suspicion. Her older sister had always gotten what—and whom—Amelia herself had wanted first. Amelia had considered employment with Pinkerton's, if they would take her. It was the most challenging job open to a woman of strong will. But she had decided against applying; she had been tired of hand-me-downs.

"Don't look at me like that!" Victoria said chidingly. "I didn't have an affair with the man, I just saw him once. I admit he was quite dashing in those days, though—and he wasn't a drunk."

For a time, hidden beneath a tarp of sleep, images crossed Farley's mind, of when he hadn't been a drunk. He wished they had lasted. The next time he opened his eyes, the tent was hot inside and sunlight stabbed him. He was sick. His nerves were all sharp inside like barbed wire.

Amelia was kneeling by his side, wiping his forehead with a cool cloth. "There, there," she murmured, "you will get over this."

His eyes were scarlet slits of agony. "I was going to sober up myself, when this was all over," he said.

"And that would be a little too late, wouldn't it, Marshal?" Amelia said testily.

"Tarnation!" Farley moaned. "There's not a damned thing I can do except get myself hung. Maybe I don't want to uphold the law, or take care of this godforsaken town, or live. Give me a drink."

"Really, Marshal, you're whining."

"You'd whine, too, if you was me," Farley said sullenly. "You don't know what it's like."

"Oh, I have a few ideas. I have uncles that drink, and a father. One of my McCoy uncles died of it. He gave up, just as you have been doing."

Farley gritted his teeth. Sour sweat beaded his forehead. He hadn't realized how much the drink had taken him, wrapping him up worse than the ropes that bound him. It wasn't until he was shut off that he knew he hadn't been coasting along. He'd lied to himself about that.

If only he could make it through this day, he'd be himself again. But, God, he couldn't do it. His mind turned sly. "Where's the other one—your sister?"

"She has other business to tend to, but don't go getting any ideas." Amelia palmed the tiny derringer that swung power to her side.

"You wouldn't," he said.

"I might. Seems to me if you stay drunk, you might as well be dead, for all the good you can do."

A spasm shook Farley. He retched. Amelia shoved a shallow basin under his unshaven chin. He was dying, and she was as cool and unruffled as a mother tending her baby.

He felt shame replace his rebellion. She was, damn her, right. He had to get sober if he was going to be any kind of a man or marshal, and he hadn't been doing it on his own.

Time stretched out like the rawhide holding a bucking bronc, taut and long and threatening to snap with strain.

Farley was feverish. He wasn't sure what day it was. He dreamed, frightening dreams with O'Dell's leering face coming at him, dreams of the hangman's noose replaced by giant locomotive engines rushing toward each other on a collision course. He dreamed of blood and murder and death and snakes crawling all over his belly.

When he awoke the next time, Amelia was cradling his head in her arms. His blue eyes opened. They were blue now, not blood-red, though his eyelids were puffy.

"What time is it?"

"Four in the afternoon," Amelia said softly. Her voice was melodious, but it echoed in his ears.

"What afternoon?"

"September eighteenth."

"Thank God," he sighed, and drifted off again.

Later she brought tea for him. He managed to get it down without gagging. He was very weak. Amelia helped him sit up. After he had finished, he said, "I could scream for help, you know. You can't keep me here forever."

"Farley, I don't for a minute think that you would raise a ruckus. You want everyone in town to know you've been shanghaied by a couple of women? Besides, I only want you to stay here tonight," she said in a no-nonsense tone of voice. "By morning you'll be over the worst of it. Then it's up to you."

"I'm fine now—and sober. Let me go. I'm the marshal in this town, and Crush is getting pretty wild. I have a job to do."

"In the shape you're in, I doubt you could hold your own gun. You are still a sick man."

"I've managed when I was a lot sicker than this." Was it Amelia's imagination, or was there a note of bravado in his voice? A bad sign.

"If anything comes up, Gus will handle it. He's been deputized since Bad Lungs turned up missing—and good riddance. In fact, Victoria has told everyone you are out of town on important business until tomorrow, so it will look exceedingly strange if you show your face. You deputized your barkeep before you left, by the way."

"You two sisters sure you aren't brothers? I've half a mind to see if you're hiding any brass balls under those skirts," Farley complained.

"Hmmph."

"Woman, you might as well untie me, because I've got my strength back now, and those knots you fixed up aren't worth a tinker's damn."

"Neither blasphemy nor insults nor threats will work, you know," Amelia said, tightening the ropes around his hands.

"Ouch! Why the hell are you doing this?"

Amelia thought for a long time before answering. Dusk was settling over the town by now, and inside the tent the soft light played against her dark hair and the sweet curve of her cheekbone.

Finally she spoke. "I'm not sure just why, except I know you were once a highly respected lawman. I know other things, too."

Farley didn't want to listen, but he was trapped. The pain he had shoved down so far that he rarely felt it tore through him like a knife.

Amelia's voice was soft and her words simple, but he could feel tears of helplessness and rage wash over him as she spoke. She told him what she knew about Cripple Creek and how his life had taken a long, downhill slide.

"Maybe I had something to live for then," Farley said, sunk in a well of self-pity. "When Lottie ran off, I lost the only friend I ever had—"

"You have friends now, in this town. Besides my sister and myself, there is Gus, and Wade Puckins, who needs your help. Really, Farley, I hate a man who snivels."

"You don't understand," Farley shouted.

"Shush now, or we are both likely to suffer embarrassment. Can't you just see it if O'Dell were to find you here? He would get you back drinking, I have no doubt, out of pure shame. He likes you to drink, doesn't he?"

Farley knew this was so. He didn't want to know it, but deep down he did. As long as he stayed sucking on the bottle, O'Dell did own him. He'd been trying hard not to see it, but it was so.

"You know about Thaddeus Beauchamp?" Farley asked. "He killed Lottie, and I killed him, but it was murder. O'Dell could have me hung if he wants."

"Oh, so that's why you sold out to him?"

"I did not," he said hotly. "We made a deal. It was that or getting strung up, and I've done marshaling before."

"A lot of keeping the law you're doing, falling off a bar stool into Clara's bed every night."

"You are the cussedest old maid I've ever seen," Farley protested. "If you don't kill me sobering me up, you're going to have O'Dell do the killing. Can't you see there's no way out for me?"

"Maybe, maybe not," Amelia said, stubborn now. "But what about the people you've sworn to protect? What about the innocent citizens Puckins thinks will be injured over this train crash? What about the illegal boxing match? There's big trouble, and we need your help."

"Lady, let me be."

"I'm afraid I can't do that. Tonight we will stay with you ..."

Do I have any choice about that? Farley wondered.

"... and tomorrow you will find the strength to stay away from strong drink on your own, or lose your chance to be any sort of man at all."

"You always make such long speeches?" Farley asked with a wry smile, trying to get his emotions under control.

"Only about rights for women," Amelia said.

"I suppose you pity stray dogs, too," he said.

Amelia flared. "Call it pity if you want, and peg me for a speech-making do-gooder, but I am no Bible thumper or Carry Nation, contrary to slurs that have been tossed my way."

She was angry now, and perversely started to untie his bonds. The surprised expression on his face had nothing to do with relief. In fact, he felt a yawning emptiness.

"Oh, you *are* hopeless. Go, then, get out of here. Go back to your saloon. Don't help us—"

"Amelia! It's me. Victoria."

Victoria let herself in. She was breathless and upset. She had been running. She saw Amelia was freeing Farley Dant.

"Oh, you already heard the bad news. Guess we have to let you loose sooner than we expected, Farley. Gus is down by the train tracks waiting for you. Hurry."

"I didn't hear anything," Amelia said, near hysteria. "He won't help us, so I'm not going to bother—"

"Where'd you hide my Colt?" Farley said. "What the hell happened?"

"Oh, Victoria, he's been calling me a—"

"Calm yourselves, both of you!" Victoria ordered. "This is not the time for a lovers' quarrel."

"Lovers' quarrel!" Farley snorted.

"Children! Quiet! Wade Puckins has been shot through the gut. He's dying. The railroaders are forming a vigilante committee, and some man claims he saw James the telegraph man shoot Wade. I'm sure that's hogwash, but Weasel Face is backing the fellow up."

"James?" Farley was grim. "I'd bet my last drink O'Dell is behind it, or Willie Crush."

Both women stared at Farley. His unfortunate reference to betting his last drink made them realize how weak and uncertain the man still was, and this latest incident might be enough to send him back to the bottle.

Victoria handed him his holster and pistol silently.

Amelia watched him prepare to face the enraged crowd back at the tracks. He loaded his gun and checked his ammunition. His fingers were shaking, but he managed.

Armed but unshaven and unkempt, it seemed all that was moving him forward was backbone. He shuffled his feet, as if looking down at them for answers, before straightening up.

His eyes met Amelia's.

"I think I can make it, though I might get myself strung up for trying. Lots of things around here need tending to, besides me."

"Marshal," Victoria offered. "I have a gun and know how to use it. Do you need my help?"

"No. I can't accept you as an extra gun. With the way men around here are, it might cause more problems. I believe we'd do better if you stayed out of the line of fire, no insult intended."

"The odds are not good. A lot of the men are armed," Victoria said.

"I have Gus and maybe a few levelheaded citizens who don't take to lynching on my side. James had friends, too, who won't believe he did it. Who's stirring up the hanging party? That's information I could use."

Amelia felt a stab of jealousy. Farley was talking to Victoria as one professional to another. Amelia knew *she* would have taken his refusal of an extra gun personally, and Farley never would have spoken to her with the same matter-of-fact respect.

"There's a new railroader—or that's what he says he is—who got into town today. The man's name is Walt Smith, and he's been tight with Gorman ever since he got to Crush."

"A railroader? Sounds like a ringer to me," Farley commented.

"Likely," Victoria agreed. "There's been talk that Wade was going to stop the crash, so we know *why* he was shot."

"Why would they pin it on James, though? He's never done anyone dirt around here."

"My guess is that Gorman wants him out of the telegraph office. They'd been friendly, but Gus said they were quarreling about something last night."

"Anything else?" Farley asked.

"Yes," Victoria said. "This Smith fellow is great at

rousing a crowd, especially with Weasel Face to back him up. The railroaders are feeling mean. They all liked Puckins."

"Not a chance. They won't listen. You can't reason with drunks. Willie sent the Katy crew free jugs earlier, as a last celebration before the crash, so none of them are too sober."

"Well, I am," Farley said, raising his chin defiantly. Then, as an afterthought, he added, "But if your offer still stands, Amelia, I might be back later."

Chapter Fifteen

It had been a few years and a lot of miles since Farley'd seen a lynching, but it wasn't something he was about to forget in a hurry. The way a lynching happened was about like a day that unfolded all mild and sunny on the surface, only there was something different in the air, something tense and mean, and then all of a sudden a twister rolled in.

Looking back, it always seemed there should have been some way to stop it, if only you'd known what that meanness in the air was. During his drifting years, when Farley worked as lawman in a small Kansas town that couldn't get anybody else, there'd been a lynching party. It'd happened so fast; he'd seen normally sensible citizens go wild, and the horse thief strung up while they cheered. Farley'd laid down his badge right afterward.

Once a mob got worked up, Farley knew, there wasn't any way of stopping it until it had blown itself out, and likely as not, by then at least one man was dead.

The trick was, Farley thought, to tame the mob before it got completely out of control. He hoped he was not too late. Up Broadway, he could see men swarming, lighting up the street in front of the jail with torches. Railroad ties made good torches.

That meant James was locked up in jail. Thank God this jail house was made of more than chicken wire. The trouble was, even jail cells could be busted into. Besides, Weasel Face was the one who had the keys, so it wouldn't even be that hard.

If Farley's guess was right—and it wasn't a guess that took any great figuring on his part—O'Dell had given Weasel Face orders to sort of let the mob have its way.

O'Dell had not counted on Gus.

Farley saw him up there, facing down the mob with an old Sharps rifle Farley'd never seen before. The old buffalo gun was as out of date as vigilante rule, but it would put one helluva hole in a man.

It was a standoff; Weasel Face was standing beside Gus, pointing a six-shooter at him.

Usually the railroaders were not a bad lot, mostly kept to themselves, drank and sported hard when they weren't working, but without being hardcase about it. Now they were all worked up and could be tough in a fight.

Farley scanned the crowd but he didn't see Willie Crush's bowler derby—or Gorman's, either. He didn't expect to, really, any more than he expected to see O'Dell. They were wily as old foxes. It might suit all three of them to have Wade out of the way and James as well, but they would just start things and let the loco fury of the crowd

156

finish things off. Any one of them could have hired that troublemaker Victoria had spotted to stir things.

Farley heard a gruff, loud voice shout, "Hang James. Hang the telegrapher. We want the man who shot Puckins."

The others picked up the chant: "Hang James. Hang James. Hang James."

Farley was easing up behind the milling mob; it was hard to think of them as men, now that they were like one headless monster screaming away without making much sense. Worse than the chanting, they were advancing, and Gus looked whiter than a Chinaman's laundry.

The loudest man was a stocky fellow wearing Katy clothes that looked a little too stiff and new on him. He was outfitted like a railroader, but something was a little off, like slightly tainted meat. His hair was cut differently, and he had a layer of ease over his smooth-planed face.

So far the angry crowd had not taken any notice of Farley. They were too busy waiting for Weasel Face to disarm Gus.

Farley'd bought a drink for most of them, one time or another, down at the saloon, but that didn't mean they wouldn't turn on him, with all that anger roiling them up into one big boil of hatred.

Weasel Face's gun arm was edging closer to Gus, though Gus didn't flinch. Weasel Face snarled, "Drop the rifle, Gus. You ain't no lawman. I'm the law now that Dant's away."

In a pig's ass, Farley thought.

Farley elbowed his way up to where he could get a bead on Weasel Face. Some of the men beside him were armed, but none had their guns cocked—not yet. Farley cocked his. Several men nearby finally noticed him, but none were quick enough to get in his way.

Farley'd been watching and waiting for a chance to smash Weasel Face ever since he first laid eyes on him back in West. He knew that Weasel Face only talked big and had a yellow streak a mile wide. He knew it wouldn't take fists or a bullet to smash him; all Farley had to do was show him up for a coward.

"Weasel Face, drop your gun," he ordered.

The silence was loud enough to fill the night for a full Texas minute. The pistol wavered in Weasel Face's hand. Farley's voice was rough as an old cob, and shaky, too, but he said, as clearly as he could, "I'm going to count to three, and if that gun of yours isn't on the ground, I'll shoot. One . . ."

"I've got Gus covered. He's trying to stop justice."

It was a chance Farley had to take, because if the shooting started, Gus would get shot up, anyway. It was a gamble, but if he knew Weasel Face, the man would back down. Otherwise, it was all but the shouting.

"Two."

The mob held its collective breath.

"Thr—"

The gun dropped to the ground.

Farley moved in, his Colt still drawn and cocked, and took his place beside Gus, facing the mob. With his free hand he shoved Weasel Face toward the crowd.

Weasel Face stumbled to his knees like a whipped dog. He hated Dant, always had from the first. Weasel Face figured in his own mind that if it weren't for Dant, he would be marshal of Crush and have his run at the saloon, instead of just being a deputy.

Besides, O'Dell would be mad about this. It wasn't that Weasel Face had anything against the telegrapher they were going to string up, but O'Dell had given Weasel Face orders on what to do, and he had been doing fine. That's what counted.

Dant was supposed to be away, and O'Dell had said something about killing two birds with one stone, something Weasel Face didn't understand but didn't have to, as long as things went the way O'Dell wanted them to go. Weasel Face was just following orders. Everything was sweet until Dant showed up.

Weasel Face stumbled to his feet and whined, "I'll get you for this, Dant."

The sound of the crowd swelled once more, dwarfing the guns Gus and Farley had readied. "Marshal, we don't want to hurt you or Gus, but we will if you try to stop us. Ain't that right, boys?"

A cheer went up, and torches waved in the air.

"Give us James, the man who shot Wade Puckins."

Smith; Victoria had said the rabble-rouser's name was Walt Smith.

Farley wished his brain was working better. It was clear, all right, not fuzzy like when he was drunk, but every thought seemed to turn inside the way a stubborn screw does, corkscrewing around without tightening up.

Instinct, though—Farley had that going for him He'd tamed mobs a few times, only there was no taming them, not really. A mob was like a snake, and even if you cut off its head, it could keep going. But if you got its tail wrassling with its head, you stood a chance.

Trouble was, Farley didn't have time to think it out slowly, and the men were moving in. Farley could smell the whiskey on their breath. They were not, he judged, inclined to be sensible.

He motioned for Gus to move forward a pace, as he was doing. This surprised the shouting man, who expected them both to retreat. "We are all friends of Wade Puckins, aren't we?" Farley shouted.

"Darned right."

"We'll kill the man who shot him—"

"Give us the murderer."

"Hold it there, boys!" Farley said, straining to keep his voice level. "Is Wade dead yet?"

"Good as," a young brakeman with a peach-fuzz mustache said. "James gut shot 'im, and he's dying."

"Any of you tried talking to Puckins?"

"I did," Smith yelled, half turning so the crowd could see the burning intensity in his eyes. "He told me it was up to us to get James, the man who shot him—"

"Hold on." Farley grabbed the brakeman and spun him around so he was facing Smith. "Is this the man who told you about what happened?"

The young man's voice broke as he said, "Yeah, that's him. He said he saw it all, and James shot Puckins."

"What of it? I saw it. Come on, boys, there's all of us against the marshal and his friend. Let's hang the murderer. Let's hang him for Wade. We always take care of our own."

Farley thrust the kid closer to Smith. "How well do you know this man who calls himself Walt Smith?"

A groan erupted from the crew. They were getting antsy. They had been full of booze and high spirits when Wade was shot. Then they got riled with a different kind of spirit, a killing spirit, and they wanted some action.

The young brakeman said, "Marshal, Smith is a railroader, same as me. You so blind drunk that you can't tell?"

"I guess so," Farley drawled. "I know a lot of you, drank with a lot of you, saw you around the saloon. Hell, I like Wade Puckins as well as any man I've run across."

A torch came close enough to Farley's face so he could smell the smoke. He felt its heat. "Let's go on with it. Out of the way, Marshal—"

The barrel of Gus's Sharps rifle pushed the man back.

The rest of the men grumbled and started shoving forward. Time was running out. A crowd was finicky like that, and one movement was enough to push them over the edge to violence. Farley didn't know if he could stop them now. He pointed his pistol above their heads and fired twice.

"That leaves four bullets, gentlemen."

Those in back still grumbled boldly, but the men in front quieted down.

"I don't know Smith from Adam, but I'd guess he ain't one of you, not a workingman, a railroader. Oh, he might be a company man, a stockholder's man, but he ain't one of you. Look at him close. Why, he ain't been around long enough to be a good friend of Wade's."

"When did he show up, anyways?"

"Before the shooting, blockhead. He saw it happen."

"He on your part of the crew?"

"I thought he was with you."

Farley could sense a change in the crowd, a seed of doubt creeping in as they whispered to one another. This was the time.

He told Gus quietly, "You take it from here, friend. Drinks are on me—if you can't get 'em down to the saloon and away from the jail."

Gus cleared his throat. He did it again, louder.

"Hmph. Hey, boys, I don't know about you, but I got to wet my whistle. Seems you could talk this out better down at the saloon. Hell, last we heard, Wade wasn't dead yet. Maybe we ought to drink to him, and drinks are on the marshal."

Walt Smith was shaken, but he gave it another try. "You going to be bought off like this? Hell, I'll buy the whiskey once we get the hanging done—"

"Sure you will," a stoker said, "with whose money?"

"You reckon he's from the St. Louis office?"

"His overalls do look kind of shiny new."

Farley shouted above the din, "Why don't you all go have a drink to old Wade. You know Wade would be the last one who would want any of you to get hurt. He wouldn't want a hanging. He's a peaceable man."

"That's right," he heard several of the men say, slightly sobered. "Wade was always against hangings."

As a crowd they had lost their force and drifted off in ones and twos. Farley patted Gus on the back and said, "Looks like the saloon is going to be busy tonight."

"And them all ripe for more trouble," Gus commented. "You want this badge back yet?"

"No," Farley said. "You'll need it. Besides, you deserve to wear it, whether you want it or not."

Gus shrugged. "I want it, all right. I'm not sure about deserving it. One thing you maybe ought to know."

"If it's about earlier today, I don't want to know it," Farley said. "It was the sorriest trick another man ever pulled on me, sending me down there to those two women."

"It's about the rifle, and my pistols that got stole from the saloon. I'm going to need a six-shooter, to keep the peace tonight. I think either Evelyn or Madame Hortense took my real guns."

"Glad you had the old rifle. It did the job. I'll check into the theft later, but I'm not sure what I can do about it. Here, take Weasel Face's pistol. He's not getting it back."

"Obliged," Gus said. "Funny thing about the Sharps, though...."

"What's that?"

"I haven't had ammunition for that old thing in years. It wasn't loaded."

"Get out of here before I wish I was still a drinking man," Farley said.

After Gus left, Farley regretted telling Gus that, because the craving for a drink was eating him up inside. He tried to reason it out, but one part of his brain told him he deserved a drink because he had just stopped a hanging.

He knew where some whiskey was kept: in the bottom drawer of his desk. He eased into the new jail house and sat down. His knees suddenly felt like water. His hands shook with the effort of holding them back from that desk drawer.

James called from the jail cell, "They gone for good?"

"I'm not sure," Farley said. "But they are gone for now. You ready to tell me what happened?"

"I didn't shoot him," James said, eyes bugging out of his head with fear.

"I figured that. Were you around?"

"Close enough," James said. "A telegram came in from West for Puckins, and since the office was closing down, I took it down to the tracks to him. They were all drinking, except for Wade, who don't drink much. He was sitting over by himself, by one of those engines they're going to crash."

"You see who shot him?"

"No. I was just getting near him when the bullet whistled by. Lucky I wasn't shot myself. Next thing I knew, that guy who calls himself Smith was saying I did it."

"What happened to the gun that shot him?" Farley asked.

"There was a gun, all right. Smith picked it up off the ground. Marshal, I guess I ought to tell you, it was my gun, but I didn't do it."

"James, I'm inclined to believe you, but it might look bad for the judge."

"If I get a judge's trial," James added bitterly.

"Where was your gun, before it showed up after Wade was shot?" Farley asked.

"Back in the telegraph office, where I always keep it. I can't see no reason toting it, Marshal. I'm a poor shot at best. I can't see beyond my nose, to tell the truth. That's why I like Morse code and being behind a desk, where I can see things proper."

"Well, I couldn't see that you had any reason to shoot Wade, but there are those who had plenty. Seems like there's been a rush of gun stealing going on. Any idea who might have gotten hold of your gun?"

"Clive Gorman."

"I thought you and him was friendly," Farley said.

"We were, until he tried to mess with running the telegraph office. He wanted to pay me off and handle things for a few days. Marshal, I couldn't let him do that. It's my job."

"James, you got friends in Crush who might stand up for you? Be better if you know someone handy with firearms."

"There's Silas Clute and some of his workers. And Gordon Fink, who runs the shebang."

"I think I might just deputize them. Know anyone you might trust to run the telegraph until this blows over?"

"A few I'd trust, but none of them know Morse."

"Guess we'll have to think on that," Farley said. "There's damned few around here I would trust...."

"Marshal? Let me in."

"But here come one of them."

"A woman!" James squeaked. It was his life that needed protecting, and the marshal had a woman calling. James did not think it was a good sign.

Later, when Virginia rounded up some new deputies,

165

men who believed James was innocent, James pondered things over a bit.

On reflection he decided he was in no position to scorn a woman's help, especially when she knew how to use a gun and could rattle off the code almost as fast as he could.

Still, he was mighty uneasy about this whole mess. Every time he heard a whooping and hollering through the long night, he felt his neck get tight and scratchy.

He was glad to see the sun come up.

For a while there, James had thought he wouldn't live to see another day. He was a man who could live real well without surprises.

Chapter Sixteen

Throughout the night gunshots exploded.

The railroaders were wound up tighter than eight-day clocks. One of them had a fight with a cardsharper; another chased a mechanic down Broadway, shooting high but meaning it, over Snaggletooth Alice's favors. It was that kind of night.

Two of the Katy crew cornered Walt Smith down at the livery. He had hired a horse to get him out of town. He was about to see the last of Crush, Texas, and he wasn't going to compound his problems and head in the direction of West.

O'Dell had paid Walt Smith five hundred dollars up front; the other thousand he was supposed to get, he could kiss good-bye.

Smith knew that the honorable judge was as shifty a man to work for as he was mean. Killing Puckins was only half the job—and a botched one, at that. Puckins might yet live to cause trouble. It was, Smith decided, time to ride hard and fast, maybe south toward the border.

Railroad men were hardworking, hard-drinking men, but they were not generally horsemen or good shots, though many carried guns. A true railroader'd seen more of the West than any ten townsmen put together, but he was a fistfighter more than a shooter.

Besides, Smith figured the railroaders were a dumb breed, all brawn, including between their ears. If they went for the line of prime bull he had thrown at them earlier, he figured it would take them days to figure it was him, Smith, who actually had shot Puckins.

He'd be long gone, Smith thought as he saddled up a sorrel mare. He almost calculated wrong, because that's when the two railroaders hunted him down just outside the stables.

Smith saw a glint of silver in the young brakeman's hand. He didn't ask questions. He shot the brakeman clear through the chest and aimed two more shots at the fireman the crew called Tallow Pot.

"He almost got me," the fireman told Farley later. Farley had helped carry the wounded railroader over to the sawbone's office in back of the shebang, where Wade Puckins lay dying.

"All I wanted to do was fight him fair," Tallow Pot said. "I remembered how Wade felt, about guns and about hangings, but by God, I wanted to smash Smith's face in."

Farley said, "With fists like yours, you would have done some good"—Tallow Pot's hands were the size of smoked hams, and just as tough—"but you don't go up against hired guns with your fists."

"That's what my brakeman said, which is why he brought the Peacemaker along, but it happened so fast, he didn't have a chance to shoot."

"Lucky he took Smith by surprise and only caught a clean shot in his left side. Missed his lung by a good inch. He'll live."

"I'm going to round up some of the Katy crew, to go after Smith," Tallow Pot said. "The son-of-a—"

"You already got one wounded and one dying," old Doc Smithers said, breathing whiskey fumes at Tallow Pot. "I can't handle no more tonight."

Neither could Farley. He was nervous as a cat in heat. First, he needed a drink so bad, he felt like the hammers of hell were pounding at him.

Second, he had left Silas Clute and a few townsmen back at the jail to guard it. Good men, but not used to keeping the peace.

Third, he knew Crush was a powder keg that could go off at any moment. The last thing he needed was a bunch of drunk angry men chasing Smith. They were liable to end up shooting each other.

"You get your crew roused up again and I'll jail the bunch of you," Farley said. "I'll get the Texas Rangers after Smith. You tell your boys what happened, though. I'd just as soon be able to let James out of jail. He's only there for his own protection."

Wade Puckins's eyes were glazed over, but he'd been listening. He knew he was dying. He was quiet about it, though, not like the injured young fireman who cussed and thrashed about when the doc poured raw whiskey on his wound.

With the last of his energy Wade said, "Tallow Pot, I got something to say."

Doc Smithers and Farley looked at each other. They'd both heard enough dying to know that these would be Wade's last words—and that they'd come out hard, at that. Puckins was white and drawn and his breath rattled.

Tallow Pot bent over to listen. He was a big man with broad shoulders and a solid gut on him; overall, he had the looks of a big bull. It was strange to see him move so silent and gentle and grasp Wade's hand. Tallow Pot'd been with Wade since Kansas City. "Wade, I'm listening," he said hoarsely.

"We lived through a crash together, didn't we?" Wade said. It was not what he had wanted to say, but his mind was drifting.

"Sure did—"

"Never thought I'd get it this way, did I? Never ... always looked after my men, didn't I, like they was my own ... it's been my life, the railroad ... don't let any of my boys die ... tell 'em no ... no ... no!"

Farley turned his face away so he would not see the tears in Tallow Pot's eyes. He could not escape hearing the harsh sob of final loss from the big, grieving fireman. It was the only sound in the sick-smelling room until Doc Smithers clunked a bottle of red-eye on the table. The physician uncorked it, took a swig, and handed it to Farley.

The bottle felt solid and cool in Farley's hand. His fingers caressed the smoothness of the glass, memorizing its curves.

Without lifting the bottle, Farley swallowed so hard that his Adam's apple bobbed. He tasted a salty, sad taste in his mouth. He knew how the whiskey would taste, that first snort, all warm and glowing, taking the sad taste away.

Farley raised the bottle. The whiskey smell tickled his nostrils stronger than any woman's perfume, but it was cloying and sickening at the same time. One swallow and the sick-sad feeling would go away, though.

Farley's stomach rumbled. Barbed-wire nerves jangled up inside him. His eyes twitched with wanting the whiskey so bad.

He felt like a puppet he saw one time in a traveling show. The puppet jerked its arms and legs every time the puppet master pulled a string. The whiskey was the string—one sip and Farley'd be jerking to a cruel puppet master's tune. God, he knew it, but it was hard.

Farley closed his twitching eyes so tightly, he saw a red glow in front of them. Then, suddenly, he swung the lip of the whiskey bottle away from his quivering mouth. "I got work to do."

His voice croaked.

He shoved the bottle into Tallow Pot's hands. "Tell your crew what happened. Tell them to look after themselves and let the Rangers catch Smith."

Farley stumbled out of the doctor's office.

Within seconds he was running down the street, running so fast that a sweat broke out all over his body. He didn't stop until he reached Amelia's tent.

* * *

By sunup, September nineteenth, it was exactly twenty-seven hours, twenty minutes, and forty-five seconds since Farley'd had his last drink—not that he was counting.

The McCoy sisters also had had a rough night.

Victoria had relayed orders between the jail house—Silas Clute was in charge of the night watch there—the saloon, and the marshal. Farley stayed with Amelia in the tent. Sometimes he slept. Sometimes he woke and raved like the devil himself was standing on his shoulder taunting him.

Several hours before the break of day, all the reports Victoria brought back from Crush were good. The saloon was winding down its rush business. Only a few stray shots were heard disturbing the peace, and that was business as usual in Crush these days. Most of the railroaders were back at the caboose they were calling home. The jail house was silent and secure.

"—And I am going to get some sleep," Victoria said.

"Shh, Sister. Farley just dozed off, and if I don't get some sleep myself, I'll be in no shape to take pictures. I have to get ready to photograph the crash."

"You and your pictures," Victoria said, exasperated more from the habit than real conviction. "I have real work to do. There are some men out there I'm sure are on Pinkerton's list, and I am going to bring them in."

Victoria went on, sleepily detailing her plans as she got ready for bed, but Amelia was already asleep. Farley was snoring in the other bedroll. Shaking her head, Victoria crawled in beside Amelia and promptly fell asleep herself.

Clarence, who was still in charge of the upstairs rooms at Dant's, was not happy when Farley strode in demanding a bath. "But, Marshal, ain't but a wink into the day, and this ain't a Saturday no how."

"It's Friday morning and I expect a bath. Also, Clarence, fetch me my clothes from upstairs, and anything else that belongs to me."

The wizened clerk's eyes widened enough so his wrinkles bunched up around them. "You want me to get your clothes from that woman's room!"

"That's what I said. Now."

"But, Marshal, she ain't goin' to like it. Women and me don't get along too well, and well, since you're not rightly my boss—"

"This boss enough for you?" Farley asked, pointing his Colt at Clarence.

Farley got his bath and clothing.

"Seems like everybody's been tattling on me," Farley later told O'Dell casually, at the new jail.

Farley sat with his worn boots up on the desk, his pot-metal badge pinned prominently on the front of his clean vest. Further, the clean vest was worn over a clean shirt. His trousers didn't look too shabby, either.

Worst of all, as far as O'Dell was concerned, Farley's

eyes were clear. He looked reasonably sober, and he had not even stood up when Sherm walked in.

"Not tattling, Farley, just letting me know what's going on in this town. Boy, I'm disappointed in you."

"For stopping a lynching?"

O'Dell squirmed a little. "Hell, you know me better than that."

"I do?"

"I mean, for turning loose a good thing. Why, that Clara is a-sobbing her heart out back at the saloon. Thought you were against breaking little ladies' hearts."

"And just when did Clara become a lady?"

"Hell, Dant, I didn't come to talk about your love life. I have other business, and I don't like what happened here last night. Could give me a bad name."

"I sure hope so."

"Listen here, boy, and listen good. All of a sudden you're getting a bit too uppity for a man in your position, if you get my drift. Tomorrow is the big day. All right, maybe the railroaders got a little hasty, and that stranger was the one who shot Puckins, maybe over an old grudge. Maybe you did right. But you had no right to free James, on your word, without talking to me first, and that's a fact."

"I don't hold with keeping an innocent man locked up."

"Letting him out is stirring up trouble, with old Puckins being buried today. Besides, what happens to him doesn't make any difference to our arrangement. Who cares?"

Farley did, but he was too sick to argue. For some reason he thought of what Amelia always said, and repeated it. "Don't shilly-shally around with me, Sherm. James is free and there's not one railroader who thinks he shot

Puckins, not in the cold light of day. Shall I tell the Katy crew who I think sent Smith here and why?"

"But it's bygones now. What we got to think about is the big day tomorrow. I don't want you interfering. You keep the peace—and show your hero face. I want you right up in the front of spectators when those engines start steaming."

"Oh, I'm going to do my job, just as James is going to do his at the telegraph office. And I'm going to have my own deputies help me, not yours. You want things different, we'll shoot it out to see who wins. You got that, Sherm?"

O'Dell's face turned a brighter red than was normal, even for a porker like him. His liverish lips parted and drew together without letting any sound out but a huff. His brown eyes gleamed as moistly as fresh manure. He loosened his tight collar.

Finally he leaned over the desk, pushing Farley's boots aside. He stared at the marshal he was no longer sure he owned. All he needed was another twenty-four hours and they could all be damned—Farley, Willie Crush, Sylvester back in New York, and the whole damned town.

With great effort he quelled his anger. He tried for a grin, managed a grimace. "I'll be at the saloon conducting a little business. No sense in us fighting, Dant, no sense at all. You made a bargain, and I know you're a man of honor. You'll honor your part of the deal. Meet me later and we'll drink on it huh? Just like old times."

"Old times are gone, Sherm," Farley said. More astonishing, he suddenly realized he meant it.

"Yes," O'Dell agreed pompously, "and a good thing these days that a man can't get away with cold-blooded murder."

175

"Right," Farley agreed. "Like you say, this is 1896. Everything's different from what it was. I'm getting kind of modern myself, Sherm. Hell, I'll plunk myself right here at the marshal's office. I mean, these newfangled lawmen don't run a town from a saloon anymore, and thanks to you, looks like I'm one of them."

Sherm had a comeback, but he stifled it. Twenty-four hours. He turned to go. He was uncomfortably aware that his three-piece suit was too tight. He was uneasy.

Still, this was his deal. Farley's couldn't queer it now. It would work out. If Farley was going to act like a respectable lawman, why then, Farley'd be keeping Gorman and the fight fans mighty busy while Sherm tended to the velvet.

Yes, it would all work out for the best.

But Sherm couldn't help thinking that once he was on his way, he might make good his threat and let the Texas Rangers *and* the federals know that the man Farley'd shot back in West was a no-account drifter, not the bank robber Deadeye Dick.

Of course, where Sherman O'Dell was going, the news might take a while to catch up with him, but sooner or later he would have the satisfaction of knowing that Farley'd been hung. Yes, he believed that would be most satisfying.

One thing O'Dell always hated was a man who pretended to be honest. It was his maxim that you could always trust a thief more easily than an honest man. With a thief you knew what he wanted and where you stood. Take an honest man, now, and you never knew what the damned fool would do.

Give me the Gormans and Sylvesters of this world, Sherman O'Dell thought, *or the sniveling marks like the Widow Walker, and I can get along real pretty. Getting tied up with Farley might have been a mistake, but he'll get his yet. By this time tomorrow ...*

Chapter Seventeen

Farley now had fifty-five hours, twenty-seven minutes, and thirty-five seconds between him and his last drink. Not that he was counting, he thought wryly as his fingers slid over the worn gold of the pocket watch Lottie had given him in another lifetime.

It was almost high noon, September 20, 1896.

The big day had arrived. Since first light, men had been busy setting up—food tents, makeshift land-sales offices, portrait photographer's headquarters. Waco's Jervis Deane spotted the opportunity to make a buck and cordoned off the area to keep spectators a hundred feet from the train crash, except for the press and visiting dignitaries.

On the other side of town, down from Dant's, away from the tracks, men were also setting up. Gorman had hired two tow-headed kids as runners who would dash from the telegraph office to the boxing arena up until the moment the fight started. Odds for the bet were set at sixteen to one as of noon. Everybody loved Gentleman Jim, but that could change.

Through O'Dell, Gorman had hired some rougher hands who would keep the fans in line. Over a hundred associates of Sylvester McCoy's were expected in from back East. Rumor had it that Bat Masterson himself might show up, but it was unsubstantiated.

The official trainers and referees for the match were scouting out the raised platform where the contenders would battle it out. The ropes were not yet up around the ring. They would be a last-minute addition.

Townsfolk told Farley that Gentleman Jim Corbett had arrived in town late the night before, though they didn't get a close look at him. He had stayed at Dant's Saloon and Dance Hall, going directly to his room with his entourage. Some said that Clara had knocked on his door and offered him her services but was rebuffed. Corbett, from all reports, was being reclusive, refusing to glad-hand around the Crush.

Alf Larson, the contender, was different, and Farley wondered about this. Victoria, who was proving to be an invaluable source of information, reported that Alf bought the bustling saloon a round of drinks and danced with the painted ladies, boasting that it took a man and a half to go up against Corbett.

Farley said, "I don't get it at all. First off, I never heard of Alf Larson, and even if I had, I can't see him being so folksy around town. A fighter's supposed to be in training before a big match."

"What match?" Victoria said, suddenly sarcastic. "All

of us know that there are no prizefighting matches in the state of Texas."

Farley groaned. "Telling a man he can't watch or bet on a fight is taking away his rights."

"And the law is the law—or is it? Have you decided just whose law you are upholding yet? O'Dell's or the law of the state of Texas?"

"I'm trying to do my best," Farley said, angry. He was sober but still shaky. The responsibilities of the day were weighing heavy on him. "Just how much law-keeping do you expect one man to do? I have my hands full keeping the peace with the mob showing up for the great Crush crash. Besides, we can't prove anything yet." He changed the subject abruptly. "That sister of yours have her camera handy?"

"She's taking pictures of the people coming in on the excursion trains, and the crew readying the big Baldwin engines."

Stroking his chin—it was freshly shaved and he had the nicks to prove it—Farley said, "Does she know whose portraits we need?"

Victoria ticked them off. Sherman O'Dell was first on the list, followed by characters about whom Victoria had vague suspicions.

"Tell her to get a photograph of Gentleman Jim while she's at it," Farley said. "I won't get a chance to see him."

"Marshal, that's just like a man," Victoria replied "Amelia has more important things to record."

"Just tell her to do it, or ask her for me," Farley said tensely. "I have my reasons."

Just then Silas Clute came rushing up the street from the telegraph office. His face was stretched out in awe. "Marshal, you ain't never seen anything like that place. I never seen so many people crowded into one office in my life. It's about like a whole herd of beef stomping into one boxcar. I never!"

"Did you send my telegram?"

Silas shuffled his feet, and an awe-shucks look replaced his amazed surprise. "I was in line," he said, "but there weren't no way. 'Sides, James said you'd better get this one pronto."

Farley took the flimsy telegram message and unfolded it. His eyes narrowed. After he read it, he crumpled it up and stuck it in his back pocket.

Victoria started to ask, "What's—"

"Just a few fireworks I've been expecting." Farley's voice was deadly level. "Seems the Texas Rangers have gotten wind of the prizefight, and they don't like it. They're threatening to pay us a little visit."

"If you tell me not to worry my pretty little head, I'll scream," Victoria said with a scowl.

"Marshal, what do we do? I mean, me being chief deputy and all?"

"I'd rather—well, I trust you two, but I'd just as soon we kept this to ourselves. The only way we can pin anything on O'Dell is if he's caught in the act, so to speak."

"Where does that leave you?" Victoria asked.

Farley shrugged and smiled weakly. "Buried just a little deeper," he said. "Silas, when you get a chance, you might as well try to get that telegram out for me again."

181

Silas shook his head sadly without answering. He had trouble understanding Marshal Dant. He had liked the man all right, without respecting him, when Dant was running the saloon and playing at law.

But now Dant wasn't drinking, and he was flat out planning on telling those big law keepers from the state and the government that he wasn't no hero but a common murderer. It just didn't make sense to Clute.

Over the last few days, since that lynching party, Silas Clute had come to respect Crush's marshal. There was no way he wanted to send that telegram, but orders were orders.

There was nothing O'Dell enjoyed more than making collections, unless it was spending them. This was his day and not too hot for September. He was glad. The heat always made him sweat something awful.

Today he had some walking to do, and he didn't want any sweat to mar his sartorial splendor. He was wearing a new pearl-gray suit, freshly tailored, nice but not too flashy. One thing O'Dell didn't want to do was stand out in the crowd.

And what a crowd it was getting to be! Some of those excursion trains had made stops right in Crush proper. Others discharged their passengers as far away as West, and the people were flocking in by buggy and even on foot.

Naturally there were more men—they were more keen on this sort of thing—but some of them had brought along the wives and children. Why, it was a veritable stampede of humanity rushing in for the spectacle.

O'Dell estimated that most of them had no idea at all about the fight. Most of them just wanted to see a show. The bettors and fight people looked different, more shifty and excited around the eyes, not so country-wholesome.

But O'Dell was about to pull one over on them—country yokels and fight fans and bettors alike. Every time he thought of it, a silent chuckle ran through him, making his stomach quiver like calves'-feet jelly.

His good feelings got better when he collected the money from Gorman down at the ring. "We agreed," he told Clive, "that the best place to keep that kind of green is in the jail house safe. Hell, who knows what kind of thieves could be lurking out in the open?"

"Right," Gorman said nervously, "though I wish you'd sought off a better marshal. I never have felt like he's one of the boys."

"Oh, take it easy, Clive," O'Dell said, gently relieving Gorman of the cash sack which had been hand-carried down to Texas by Corbett's trainer. "I don't cotton to him much myself, but we can use him, huh?"

"We don't have a choice," Gorman said, bouncing lightly up and down and from side to side. "Minute this is over and we pay off the winner, though, we split the cream off the bet money, just like we said. Just think, Sherm, men will be placing bets from as far away as New York City!"

"Well," Sherm said into his third chin, "that velvet

comes later. What I worry about is what we got here, now and keeping it safe. Tell you what, you keep taking the bets and selling tickets, and I'll keep collecting from you up until fight time. It will all work out fine, and that's a fact."

Gorman's eyes ricochetted through the gathering crowd. "Sure," he said, distracted. More to himself, he mumbled, "That guy there never places a bet lower than five hundred dollars. . . ."

Sherm smiled. It was a trifle upsetting to think of all the money that Sylvester was collecting back East, the way they did it in betting circles, to make *his* ten percent, but it couldn't be helped.

Come to think of it, though, Sylvester would have some mighty angry bettors to answer to, not to mention Gentleman Jim Corbett. McCoy's days as a sporting man would be over.

O'Dell planned to take one hundred percent of what was here, what he could get his hands on, and he chuckled again when he thought of Gorman jiggling up and down with his pockets empty. Why, that fight might not even take place if the contenders got wind of it, and as far as O'Dell was concerned, that suited him fine.

Next stop for the judge was Dant's, which had had a big night the night before, including the gravy from Madame Hortense's end of the operation.

Then there were the sums from the plat salesman to pick up. It was nice to think that Blanche Walker would never see any of it. She'd be waiting on him that night back in West—he shuddered when he thought of the bu tons and bows the old sow affected for him—and he'd be long gone.

Yes, it was turning out to be a mighty fine day.

The man with the neatly trimmed black beard and dirty fingernails chuckled to himself. He was a loner, Deadeye Dick. He'd shot his last partner because the man had called him loco. Deadeye didn't like to be called crazy.

How could he be crazy when he had pulled one off on this whole town, hanging around and biding his time? It was a bad joke, him being a dead man and all, and Farley Dant being a hero. At first he'd been angry. He kind of cottoned to having his picture up on jail house walls— WANTED, DEAD OR ALIVE.

He was too smart for them to catch. Why, Farley'd seen him a time or two but was too pie-eyed to recognize him.

Dant had no call to claim he'd killed Deadeye Dick. It was a point of pride, and Deadeye would get even today. He made a gun with his fingers and said, "Bam!" then laughed widely. He always had been a few bales short upstairs.

The jail was getting nearly as crowded as the telegraph office. The McCoy sisters were there. Five disorderly men were locked up, and the deputies were bringing in new offenders all the time. "Just bring 'em if they're real rowdy," Farley pleaded. "Otherwise, take their guns and chase them out of town."

Sherman O'Dell was waiting for Gorman's last load of

money. Ticket sales were brisk. He already had tucked his collections bag in the safe—right under Farley's nose. This mad house suited him just fine. It would cover his actions while placing him above suspicion for the crucial hours. Gorman had no idea that O'Dell was the only one with the key to the jail house safe.

The jail was close to the mayhem. Farley and the others were heading down for the duel of the iron monsters, and O'Dell would sneak out with the loot, cool as a cucumber in the July heat.

O'Dell's presence suited Farley fine. Farley wished the Rangers would show up right now so he could dump the fight on their laps—along with O'Dell. Farley'd been praying they'd show before the crash.

He checked his watch. This time he forgot to count how long since his last drink. His face worried itself into new lines. It was time to get down to the tracks.

A new engineer had been sent in to replace Wade Puckins, and the giant Baldwin engines were being stoked up right now. Tallow Pot was shoveling coal and was urging all the men on his crew to jump from the train early.

Farley looked at Amelia, reloading her camera with more of that continuous-roll film she was always talking about—what was she starting to call the stuff, Kodak? Amelia was intent on her task. He did not look happy.

In fact, Amelia had been cold and distant to Farley today, and he knew it wasn't over the fight or which side of the law he was on or even about those pictures that meant so much to her.

With a sudden flash of revelation Farley knew it was

over the way he was working closely with sister Victoria, the Pinkerton. It occurred to him—as his heart swooped up like a hawk on the wind—that Amelia was jealous.

Self-pity stabbed him for a moment. *Why me, Lord? Why now?* But he shoved it aside with the dark but strangely comforting thought, *Maybe she'll cry for me at the hanging.*

Chapter Eighteen

Amelia was armed and ready, her Hawk-Eye fully loaded. Let that other photographer make money taking old-fashioned portrait photographs with his daguerreotype. Money wasn't what she was interested in. She was going to get action shots. Today would make her career.

She focused all her attention on the events ahead. She had to get the crash photographs, then rush down to the boxing arena.

She did not want to miss a thing—except Farley Dant. He was sober, all right, and behaving like a man with a mission, but he was a little too friendly with Victoria for her liking. It made her angry; after all, she had done a good thing for him: getting him off the bottle.

The two of them—the marshall and the Pinkerton—were downright cozy, in fact, when Amelia had last seen them back at the jail, flipping through stacks of wanted posters. Well, she had her own business to tend to.

There were upward of thirty thousand people here—

Crush was a good name for the town, Willie Crush or not. They were packed in as tight as canned peaches, the larger group by the tracks and the smaller but more avid one by the arena.

Although Amelia did not know it, Farley kept hoping the population would swell by another twenty-five men or so. He kept hoping the Texas Rangers would ride into town before the prizefight started.

They should have his telegram by now, confessing to the murder of Thaddeus Beauchamp. Farley had nothing left to lose by turning O'Dell in. He should have done it years ago, when O'Dell ran with the Slades.

Farley was sober, all right—and not liking it much.

He had a weight of worry on his shoulders, and not on his own account, though the thought of his own hanging crossed his mind a time or two.

The new engineer the Katy had brought in was overconfident, not expecting trouble. Every story Wade had told about boilers exploding came back to Farley.

He didn't have time to worry about O'Dell, or the illegal prizefight, right now. Victoria had promised she'd keep an eye on the fat judge. Farley needed to get down and see the crash spectators.

God knows, he'd pleaded with Willie Crush one last time to call off the big show, but Willie had chomped his cigar and said, "I don't have time to listen. This is going to be the greatest thing these people have ever seen, and I'm not going to disappoint them. Hell, most of them paid the Katy two dollars to get here."

Now, the best Farley could do was to keep the people at a safe distance and pray for the train crew.

The minute he got out the door, he didn't like what he saw. His footsteps quickened. The train engines whistled once and started huffing.

Someone had moved the restraining ropes up fifty feet, and people were edging closer to the tracks to see better.

Up ahead of him, Farley spotted Amelia rushing in the same direction. "Miss McCoy," he called, "slow down."

Amelia kept walking.

Farley ran after her and grabbed her by the shoulder. He spun her around. "You keep away from there," he said sternly.

The noise was getting louder: escaping steam, the roar of thousands of voices, and more strangely, the beat of horses' hooves. A cloud of dust was rising over the hill behind the tracks.

"You have no right to order me to do anything," Amelia shouted at Farley. "Save it for Victoria."

Farley's attention was divided every which way—to the fight he thought was warming up at the arena, to O'Dell at the jail house, to the riders coming in, to the fiery engines getting ready to roll.

But for a split second all he could see was Amelia.

All he could think of was that this might be the last time he saw her as a free man, before the law claimed him. All he knew was that he felt for her—and damned if he could figure out why.

He pulled her close and planted a kiss square on her lips. She gasped, struggled for all of half a second, and kissed him back. It wasn't a spinster sort of kiss.

Then, just as her eyelids were fluttering closed, they

snapped open again. She stiffened and shoved him away from her so that he tripped on his own feet.

"Farley! Behind you! A man with a gun!"

He swiveled around and saw him, a man with a black beard and black eyes and a face as familiar as an old nightmare. Had he seen the man before in Crush and failed to recognize him? Had Farley been too drunk, and too stupid?

The man gunning for him looked enough like Thaddeus Beauchamp to be his double. Farley had killed him once, in legend if not in fact. Deadeye Dick.

Farley felt like he was moving through a pot of syrupy molasses. Every move he made was heavy and unreal. It was like he was looking at another man who had nothing to do with him.

He saw his own arm bend at the elbow. He saw Deadeye's fingers begin to move a moment before his own reached down to his holster. He saw himself point the barrel of his Colt right at the gunman's heart. He shot.

Blam.

Toot. Chug. Another toot.

The man fell. Passersby screamed.

The thirty-five ton Baldwins pulling their chains of gaily painted boxcars kissed cowcatchers and started backing up. The crowd roared. They were within thirty feet of the crash site.

Farley started running, looking back over his shoulder once to scream at Amelia, "Keep away from the crash! Run in the other direction. Go—go!"

Amelia stood, stunned.

Out of reflex, she picked up her Hawk-Eye and squeezed

off a shot of Deadeye Dick lying dead on the ground, his gun out of his holster but unfired. Then she picked up her skirts and raced toward the tracks. She was not about to miss the most important pictures of her career.

The two trains were backed up now, facing each other across half a mile of empty track. They were magnificent, snorting steam like fiery dragons. Engine number 999 was red with green trim, and number 1001 was red with green trim. Their diamond-shaped stacks gleamed. They were polished to a high gloss.

People shoved closer, ignoring the ropes. Amelia saw Farley running and yelling. He could not be heard against the roar of the crowd and the noise of the engines. He was waving the people back, and they were ignoring him.

Her camera in front of her, she snapped quick shots. She saw the other photographer, Jervis, ducking behind the black box of his daguerreotype, less than twenty-five feet from where the trains would collide.

In the distance the advancing horsemen crested the sloping hill. The Texas Rangers had a panoramic view of the town of Crush. They halted their mounts and thirty-five tons apiece of hot steel started groaning along the tracks, picking up speed.

The noise was deafening, but it was suddenly punctuated by the blasts from a six-shooter. Farley was jumping up and down like a maniac, firing his Colt above the heads of the crowd. Women and children screamed and started running backward; men counted the shots.

The five loaded bullets Farley had left scattered most of the crowd back about a hundred feet. His fingers fumbled as he tried to reload, but it was too late. It was all happening too fast.

The trains were careening down the tracks. Twenty miles an hour ... thirty ... forty and still picking up speed. Crewmen were leaping into the air and landing by the tracks, rolling over and over into the grass at track side.

Willie Crush and stockholders from St. Louis, watching from a safe grandstand seat, held their breath.

The trains were unmanned now and doing fifty miles an hour. The locomotives should meet with a bang, rear up, and fall over—all for a spectacular show.

They hurtled down the tracks.

They collided with a shriek of steel on steel.

There was a shower of sparks and the engines reared into the air—and then it happened. The boiler on number 999 was the first to go, exploding in a shower of steam and flying shards of metal. The mighty, roaring bang shattered eardrums.

Another explosion followed, louder than the first, as the boiler of number 1001 blew up. Boxcars climbed up on one another, disintegrating. The crowd was too stunned to move. It happened too damned fast.

Then shrieks of pain rent the air.

The spectators started running like headless chickens, pushing and shoving to get back from the fiery inferno. Children wailed and women sobbed.

A sliver of steel whistled by Farley's head, missing him by inches.

The Texas Rangers thundered down the hill.

Farley spotted a few of his deputies and members of

the Katy crew rushing to the scene of the disaster. They gathered around him. He took charge out of pure instinct. He did not have time to think.

"Get the people who aren't injured up on that slope before they trample each other. Gus, I'm glad you're here. Send a boy to get Doc Smithers. Find out if there are any other doctors here. You remember that big refreshment tent Clute's men set up yesterday? Tell them to clear it out. We'll use that for a hospital."

A man from the Texas Rangers approached Farley. "Captain Hewitt here," he said.

"Marshal Dant here," Farley replied. "I need your help. I know why you're here, and we can straighten that out later. For now, can we work together?"

"At your service, Marshal," Hewitt replied.

As a team, they got the crowd under control and made litters for the wounded. Another doctor was found to assist Smithers, who was none too sober.

Farley moved mechanically, barking out orders, clearing pathways, carrying the wounded, and safeguarding the others from mass hysteria. Volunteers were organized. In addition to the hospital tent, there were first-aid stations set up for the less seriously injured.

It was an hour before Farley had time to stop and wipe his brow. Gus found him. "Farley, you finally got a minute?" he asked.

"Yes. I think we have things under control now. There are a few dead, but I think the rest of them will make it. Damn Willie Crush and his big promotion. What's up?"

"Clute's been taking care of things back at the jail. A few things I have to tell you, though. O'Dell was leaving town when Victoria cornered him. She's a Pinkerton—can you believe that? A woman?"

Farley said, "I knew."

Gus's mouth worked on something before he managed to blurt out, "She cornered O'Dell trying to leave town and locked him up. I couldn't stop her. Farley, the Rangers are here, and I know what O'Dell will tell them. Farley, you have to do something, especially after you shot that fellow again."

"Doesn't seem to be much I *can* do."

"Yes, there is," Gus said. "I have a horse ready for you—and some cash, too. Get out of here. Make a run for it. Hell, Farley, it isn't but a day or so's ride to the border."

It was tempting, Farley's throat still itched every time he thought of that rope. To run away one last time ... He cleared his throat. "You seen Amelia?" he asked.

Gus lowered his eyes. "I haven't. Listen, Farley, I better tell you before someone else does. Clute heard that the photographer was hurt bad."

"How bad?"

"Dead, I heard," Gus mumbled.

Farley turned away.

Gus came after him. "Farley, get out of here, please," he begged.

Farley just shook his head. His voice was lifeless. "Get Captain Hewitt and tell him about the fight—that one's my fault, too. Tell him to take over. I guess he knows about the murder back in West ... you might as well tell him I killed another man today. Tell him I'm not running on him."

Gus kept protesting, but Farley kept walking. He didn't know where he was heading, but his feet carried him back toward the jail house.

It's all over but the shouting, he thought.

It would be a cruel joke, he thought, to be locked up in his own jail with O'Dell.

By the time Farley crossed the threshold of the jail house, he felt so removed that he didn't listen when O'Dell started blabbering from behind bars.

Victoria was there, and she was glowing, but that didn't register, either. In her hand she had a stack of wanted posters they had gone through earlier on the desk, and a telegram. She was scribbling a message on a sheet of foolscap.

She looked up. "Oh, Farley, isn't it wonderful? I've nailed at least three of the men on Pinkerton's list—I'm sure they will have to give me that assignment I wanted. San Francisco, here I come."

"How can you—What about—Don't tell me—"

"Clam yourself, Marshal," Victoria said just as Captain Hewitt gravely walked through the door. "Amelia will be along directly. Poor thing, she twisted her ankle."

"You mean, she's all right?" Farley's jaw dropped.

"I just told you she twisted her—"

Farley reeled back against the bars of the cell and leaned heavily against them. His voice was barely a whisper. "I heard the photographer—"

"Oh, Jervis, the photographer from Waco. The doctor said he might live. Did you know him? Farley, you look positively ill."

"Let me out!" O'Dell bawled to Captain Hewitt. "I'm a judge—the honorable of West—and these people are murderers and thieves."

"We'll see about that," Hewitt said grimly. "Marshal Dant, I have some questions for you. First, are you aware that prizefighting is illegal in the state of Texas and that the governor sent us?"

"I knew—"

"Captain," Victoria said, interrupting, "perhaps we should talk privately. I am a Pinkerton. Here are my papers of identification. There are some serious matters that brought me here, and which I trust will be of interest to you."

She adroitly took the captain's arm and led him outside. O'Dell yelled after them, but they disappeared from earshot.

"I'll split fifty-fifty with you, Dant," O'Dell whined. "I've got money. Quick man, let me out of here. I can explain everything. I was going to split with you all along, and that's a fact...."

He droned on as Farley sank into a chair and propped his feet up on the desk. His head was spinning. Clute was standing in the middle of the room, his eyes downcast.

Amelia is alive, Farley thought numbly. *Alive to see me hang.*

His hand was within reach of the drawer that held his whiskey bottle, but he didn't reach for it. Instead he unholstered his Colt and set it up on the desk. He leaped back and fiddled with the piece of potmetal pinned over his heart. He unfastened the clasp and set it up beside his gun.

Clute stood watching, miserable. He wanted to say something but was afraid to.

Farley waited, his eyes half closed. He was ready for the Rangers. Perhaps it was just as well. He'd had a good run, better than most. Hell, if he'd lived, chances are he'd dream up some way to ruin Amelia's life.

The bustle outside had died down. Those people who hadn't gotten hurt were flocking out of Crush, by buggy and by train and on foot. O'Dell was beating on the cell bars, but except for that, it was almost peaceful— almost.

Farley must've dozed, because the babble of feminine voices interrupted his dream. Amelia's voice bubbled with joy. Victoria laughed and was answered by a deeper, more masculine rumble. Hewitt.

Farley opened his eyes reluctantly.

The McCoy sisters entered the marshal's office flanking Captain Hewitt.

As they faced Farley their laughter died away.

Victoria said, "Sleeping on the job, Marshal Dant? You might get your feet on the floor and stand up. The captain has a few words he wants to say to you."

Clute, who had been standing by all along, slunk over to a corner. He couldn't figure out what was going on. He'd never seen a man brought in like this before.

Farley slowly lowered his worn boots to the floor and stood up. He gestured to the gun and the badge on the desktop. He started to put his arms up in surrender—just as James came running in.

"Miss McCoy, I got what you nee— What's going on? Oh, Marshal, apologies that the telegraph machine broke down and I never did get to send that message Clute brought over. You hear me, Marshal, I never did send that telegram for you...."

James was practically yelling, and if that telegram hadn't reached anyone, then—

O'Dell called out, "Dant's a murderer, and I can prove it. He killed a man named Beauchamp and then set himself as marshal—"

"Oh, shut up!" Victoria said.

Amelia stepped forward and took the hands Farley was beginning to raise and clasped them in her own. "Oh, Farley," she said, "let Captain Hewitt thank you properly. I know how modest you are, but the Texas Rangers are grateful for all your help."

"They are?" Farley gulped.

"Yes, sir," Captain Hewitt said. "And I'll mention you to the governor in my report. All that hoopla about a prizefight—and it never was going to take place. Wish I'd gotten a gander of that ringer they brought in for Corbett. I bet Gentleman Jim is going to laugh his head off back in New York when he hears about it. Ha, ha—well, I'll tell the governor in such a way that he won't be embarrassed. Of course, we were at the right place at the right time, with those boilers exploding. Yes, I'll put that in my report—"

"He killed a man. I'm innocent! Let me out," O'Dell screamed, his face purpling. His pearl-gray suit no longer looked pristine. A button had popped in front.

"Sir," Captain Hewitt continued, "I'll leave you and this Pinkerton to deal with Shirley O'Day ..."

199

Victoria smiled broadly. Farley blinked. Amelia winked at Farley.

"... and as for the drifter you shot today, Miss Amelia explained about how she saw it all, and it couldn't be helped. I've had to shoot a man or two myself, and I know how it makes you feel, but Marshal, I hope you don't hang up your badge over it. Looks like this town needs a good lawman."

Epilogue

Amelia Bloomer McCoy and Marshal Farley Dant saw Victoria off at the new train station. Silas Clute was there to say good-bye, as was James the telegrapher and Gus the barkeep.

Dant's Saloon and Dance hall was closed. As soon as some legalities could be cleared up, it would be reopened as Crush's first hotel. The downstairs would offer libations for the men who drank. Dant wasn't one of them.

The town was peacefully building. A few men were working to clear away the remaining rubble from the crash.

Silas had turned in his deputy's badge. He was back to supervising—or would be, as soon as he said farewell to Victoria McCoy.

There was quite a civic fund for town improvements—enough for a granite town hall and a courthouse. It would not, alas, be ready in time for O'Dell's trial.

James was sorry to see Victoria go. "You've been an education, Miss McCoy," he said. "Why, one of these days we might even hire a woman as a telegrapher's assistant."

"You do that, James," she said, bussing him on the cheek. He blushed. "But don't let any of them receive messages like the ones we got from my Uncle Sylvester."

He stammered a reply. Those had been hard for his tender eyes to take—and there was no way he could have delivered them, anyway. They were addressed to Clive Gorman, and he had quietly left town, heading due west.

Victoria regally shook hands with Farley. "If you are ever interested in Pinkerton's, I could give them a recommendation," she said.

"Thank you, ma'am, but I have a town here to clean up," Farley said. A few other passengers waiting for the train, notably Evelyn and Clara, shot him looks of pure venom.

"And as for you, little sister," Victoria said as the train chugged into the station, "perhaps when you come to your senses, you will join me in San Francisco as well."

"Perhaps," Amelia said with an enigmatic smile, "after I finish my new series of photographs. I'm sure they will sell, as a follow-up to my orders. Can't you just see it? 'The Taming of a Boomtown—' "

"All aboard," the conductor shouted.

Victoria gave her sister a quick hug, swung her valise up, and disappeared into the coach. As the train began to roll out of the station a single tear zig-zagged down Victoria's cheek, although she was smiling.

"Oh, Amelia! Crush, Texas," she whispered, halfway between laughter and tears. Then she turned toward her companions to see if she could spot anyone on Pinkerton's list.

MYSTIC REBEL by Ryder Syvertsen

MYSTIC REBEL (17-104, $3.95)
It was duty that first brought CIA operative Bart Lasker to the mysterious frozen mountains of Tibet. But a deeper obligation made him remain behind, disobeying orders to wage a personal war against the brutal Red Chinese oppressors.

MYSTIC REBEL II (17-079, $3.95)
Conscience first committed CIA agent Bart Lasker to Tibet's fight for deliverance from the brutal yoke of Red Chinese oppression. But a strange and terrible power bound the unsuspecting American to the mysterious kingdom—freeing the Western avenger from the chains of mortality, transforming him from mere human to the MYSTIC REBEL!

MYSTIC REBEL III (17-141, $3.95)
At the bidding of the Dalai Lama, the Mystic Rebel must return to his abandoned homeland to defend a newborn child. The infant's life-spark is crucial to the survival of the ancient mountain people—but forces of evil have vowed that the child shall die at birth.

MYSTIC REBEL IV (17-232, $3.95)
Nothing short of death at the hands of his most dreaded enemies—the Bonpo magicians, worshippers of the Dark One—will keep the legendary warrior from his chosen destiny—a life or death struggle in the labyrinthine depths of the Temple of the Monkey God, where the ultimate fate of a doomed world hangs in the balance!

Available wherever paperbacks are sold, or order direct from the Publisher. Send cover price plus 50¢ per copy for mailing and handling to Pinnacle Books, Dept.17-298, 475 Park Avenue South, New York, N.Y. 10016. Residents of New York, New Jersey and Pennsylvania must include sales tax. DO NOT SEND CASH.

WARBOTS by G. Harry Stine

#5 OPERATION HIGH DRAGON   (17-159, $3.95)
Civilization is under attack! A "virus program" has been injected into America's polar-orbit military satellites by an unknown enemy. The only motive can be the preparation for attack against the free world. The source of "infection" is traced to a barren, storm-swept rock-pile in the southern Indian Ocean. Now, it is up to the forces of freedom to search out and destroy the enemy. With the aid of their robot infantry—the Warbots—the Washington Greys mount Operation High Dragon in a climactic battle for the future of the free world.

#6 THE LOST BATTALION   (17-205, $3.95)
Major Curt Carson has his orders to lead his Warbot-equipped Washington Greys in a search-and-destroy mission in the mountain jungles of Borneo. The enemy: a strongly entrenched army of Shiite Muslim guerrillas who have captured the Second Tactical Battalion, threatening them with slaughter. As allies, the Washington Greys have enlisted the Grey Lotus Battalion, a mixed-breed horde of Japanese jungle fighters. Together with their newfound allies, the small band must face swarming hordes of fanatical Shiite guerrillas in a battle that will decide the fate of Southeast Asia and the security of the free world.

#7 OPERATION IRON FIST   (17-253, $3.95)
Russia's centuries-old ambition to conquer lands along its southern border erupts in a savage show of force that pits a horde of Soviet-backed Turkish guerrillas against the freedom-loving Kurds in their homeland high in the Caucasus Mountains. At stake: the rich oil fields of the Middle East. Facing certain annihilation, the valiant Kurds turn to the robot infantry of Major Curt Carson's "Ghost Forces" for help. But the brutal Turks far outnumber Carson's desperately embattled Washington Greys, and on the blood-stained slopes of historic Mount Ararat, the high-tech warriors of tomorrow must face their most awesome challenge yet!

Available wherever paperbacks are sold, or order direct from the Publisher. Send cover price plus 50¢ per copy for mailing and handling to Pinnacle Books, Dept.17-298, 475 Park Avenue South, New York, N.Y. 10016. Residents of New York, New Jersey and Pennsylvania must include sales tax. DO NOT SEND CASH.

DOCTOR WHO AND THE TALONS
OF WENG-CHIANG (17-209, $3.50)
by Terrance Dicks

Doctor Who learns a Chinese magician, the crafty Chang, and his weird midget manikin, Mr. Sin, are mere puppets in the hands of the hideously deformed Greel, posing as the Chinese god, Weng-Chiang. It is Greel who steals the young women; it is Greel who grooms sewer rats to do his bidding—but there is even more, much more.... Will Doctor Who solve the Chinese puzzle in time to escape the terrifying talons of Weng-Chiang?

DOCTOR WHO AND THE MASQUE
OF MANDRAGORA (17-224, $3.50)
by Phillip Hinchcliffe

It is the Italian Renaissance during the corrupt reign of the powerful Medicis. Doctor Who, angry because he was forced to land on Earth by the incredible Mandragora Helix, walks right into a Machiavellian plot. The unscrupulous Count Frederico plans to usurp the rightful rule of his naive nephew. This, with the help of Hieronymous, influential court astrologer and secret cult member. Using Hieronymous and his cult members as a bridgehead, the Mandragora Helix intends to conquer Earth and dominate its people! The question is, will Doctor Who prove a true Renaissance man? Will he be able to drain the Mandragora of its power and foil the Count as well?

Available wherever paperbacks are sold, or order direct from the Publisher. Send cover price plus 50¢ per copy for mailing and handling to Pinnacle Books, Dept.17-298, 475 Park Avenue South, New York, N.Y. 10016. Residents of New York, New Jersey and Pennsylvania must include sales tax. DO NOT SEND CASH.

EDGE by George G. Gilman

#5 BLOOD ON SILVER (17-225, $3.50)
The Comstock Lode was one of the richest silver strikes the world had ever seen. So Edge was there. So was the Tabor gang—sadistic killers led by a renegade Quaker. The voluptuous Adele Firman, a band of brutal Shoshone Indians, and an African giant were there, too. Too bad. They learned that gold may be warm but silver is death. They didn't live to forget Edge.

#6 RED RIVER (17-226, $3.50)
In jail for a killing he didn't commit, Edge is puzzled by the prisoner in the next cell. Where had they met before? Was it at Shiloh, or in the horror of Andersonville?

This is the sequel to KILLER'S BREED, an earlier volume in this series. We revisit the bloody days of the Civil War and incredible scenes of cruelty and violence as our young nation splits wide open, blue armies versus gray armies, tainting the land with a river of blood. And Edge was there.

Available wherever paperbacks are sold, or order direct from the Publisher. Send cover price plus 50¢ per copy for mailing and handling to Pinnacle Books, Dept.17-298, 475 Park Avenue South, New York, N.Y. 10016. Residents of New York, New Jersey and Pennsylvania must include sales tax. DO NOT SEND CASH.

THE DESTROYER by Warren Murphy & Richard Sapir

#19 HOLY TERROR　　　　　　　　　　(17-210, $3.50)
Maharaji Gupta Mahesh Dor has been collecting an odd assortment of nubile western nymphets and brainwashed Baptist ministers to help bring his divine message of love to the world. But it seems the would-be converts who've been having trouble buying the Blissful Master's divine bull have been turning up not-so-blissfully dead!

#21 DEADLY SEEDS　　　　　　　　　　(17-237, $3.50)
Dying billionaire agri-industrialist James Orayo Fielding has vowed to end world hunger before he croaks. And his amazing Wondergrain seems just the ticket — fantastic fodder that'll grow faster than Jack's beanstalk in any climate from desert to tundra. But when a bunch of Market-manipulating commodities brokers begins turning up dead, the botanical benefactor's Earth-saving scheme starts to stink worse than fresh fertilizer!

#22 BRAIN DRAIN　　　　　　　　　　　(17-247, $3.50)
The mysterious Mr. Gordons is a robot with a problem. He's been busy filching fresh brains from certain ex-artistic types. But even his grisly collection of gray matter hasn't supplied the avid android with the creativity he needs to decimate his sworn enemy Remo Williams.

#23 CHILD'S PLAY　　　　　　　　　　 (17-258, $3.50)
The government's Witness Protection Program has been hitting a bit of a snag of late. Despite their brand new secret identities, certain loose-lipped mob stoolies are getting blown away by a group of gun-toting adolescents. And in an effort to save face, a big-mouth Army bigwig's been pointing the accusing finger at the wrong assassins — Remo Williams and his mentor, Sinanju master Chiun!

Available wherever paperbacks are sold, or order direct from the Publisher. Send cover price plus 50¢ per copy for mailing and handling to Pinnacle Books, Dept. 17-298, 475 Park Avenue South, New York, N.Y. 10016. Residents of New York, New Jersey and Pennsylvania must include sales tax. DO NOT SEND CASH.